Alone
in My Kayak

Alone in My Kayak

By Agnes Rodli

© Copyright 1993 — Agnes Rodli

All rights reserved. This book is protected under the copyright laws of the United States of America. This book may not be copied or reprinted for commercial gain or profit. Short quotations or occasional page copying for personal or group study is permitted and encouraged. Permission will be granted upon request. Unless otherwise identified, Scripture quotations are from The New King James Version of the Bible.

Take note that the name satan and related names are not capitalized. We choose not to acknowledge him, even to the point of violating grammatical rules.

Treasure House
a division of
Destiny Image
P.O. Box 310
Shippensburg, PA 17257-0310

"For where your treasure is
there will your heart be also." Matthew 6:21

ISBN 1-56043-768-5

For Worldwide Distribution
Printed in the U.S.A.

Destiny Image books are available through these fine distributors outside the United States:

Christian Growth, Inc., Jalan Kilang-Timor, Singapore 0315	Successful Christian Living Capetown, Rep. of South Africa
Lifestream Nottingham, England	Vision Resources Ponsonby, Auckland, New Zealand
Rhema Ministries Trading Randburg, South Africa	WA Buchanan Company Geebung, Queensland, Australia
Salvation Book Centre Petaling, Jaya, Malaysia	Word Alive Niverville, Manitoba, Canada

Dedicated to
those men and women of courage
who helped to usher in
our twentieth
century.

Contents

	Preface	ix
	Introduction	xi
Chapter One	Hunger	1
Chapter Two	Fear	13
Chapter Three	Deliverance	23
Chapter Four	Learning	33
Chapter Five	Transition	49
Chapter Six	School	59
Chapter Seven	Marooned	69
Chapter Eight	Outside	83
Chapter Nine	Saved	99
Chapter Ten	Home	117
Chapter Eleven	Family	135
Chapter Twelve	Provision	155
Chapter Thirteen	Balance	171
Chapter Fourteen	Reinforcements	187
Chapter Fifteen	Revival	195
Chapter Sixteen	Ned Nusunginya	211
Chapter Seventeen	Wainwright	227
Chapter Eighteen	Endurance	243
	Bibliography	263

Preface

The well-known war corespondent Ernie Pyle identified himself as a "rabid one-man movement bent on tracking down and stamping out everybody in the world who doesn't fully appreciate the common frontline soldier."[1]

Although not expressing ourselves as strongly perhaps, we would give similar honor to heroes like Patkotak who knew how to dig a trench and hold his ground. The central figure of this story was born in the far north at a time when hunting and fishing wasn't a matter of choice. There was simply no other way to survive. The Norwegian author, Torbjørn Båtvik, visited Patkotak in 1976 and taped several hours of an interview. Later, Florence Crawford of the Apostolic Faith mission

---

1. Ernie Pyle, *Brave Men* (Henry Holt and Company, Inc., 1944), p. 5.

gave us a copy of Patkotak's testimonies printed in a 1957 issue of their publication, *The Light of Hope*. Several of those written accounts were identical to those on tape, except for the old gentleman's unpredictable shouts of praise. That his recollections hadn't changed with the years established the credibility of a keen memory.

Don Webster and Hugh Steven together with Wycliffe Bible Translators likewise permitted us to borrow from their material. Not the least, we give credit to Patkotak's son Simeon as well as other relatives and friends who not only contributed to his personal biography, but also explained more about how they lived under "the old way." Then my nephews, Ken and Ron, came to my rescue with their technical skills when I got bogged down by the manuscript itself.

I want to thank those mentioned and everyone else who offered both time and information to help round out these chapters. They join me in a heartfelt wish that our readers' lives be enriched by this chronicle of humble folks who dared to accept God's Word at face value.

Agnes Rodli

Introduction

Knud Rasmussen looked westward. Centuries ago his ancestors had traveled across northern Alaska and Canada. Years before that they had probably made their way over what is believed to have been a land bridge connecting Asia and North America.

Rasmussen's father, a Danish state-church priest, was married to a Greenlander and had chosen to minster there in her homeland. Young Knud spoke both Danish and Greenlandic. Although later enjoying the educational advantages of a well-born European, he identified more closely with his mother's people and dedicated his life to recording their customs and folklore. He began his famous journey to Siberia in winter by crossing the ice between the northwest corner of Greenland and Canada. Dogteaming his way along the upper rim of our continent, he made frequent and lengthy stops that enabled him to adapt to changes of native dialect while familiarizing himself with variances in life style and culture. Accepting Rasmussen as one of them, the people he met talked freely, contributing invaluably to his studies of the Inuit. In his journal the explorer-historian quoted a Canadian Eskimo who summed up the significance of taboos, poignantly echoing the cries of generations before him.

We fear!

We fear the elements with which we have to fight in their fury to wrest our food from land and sea.

We fear cold and famine in our snowy huts.

We fear the sickness that is daily to be seen amongst us. Not death, but suffering.

We fear the souls of the dead, of human and animal alike.

We fear the spirits of earth and air.

And therefore our fathers, taught by their fathers before them, guarded themselves about with all these old rules and customs which are built upon the experiences and knowledge of generations. We know not how or why, but we obey them that we may be suffered to live in peace. And for all our angakoks and their knowledge of hidden things, we yet know so little that we fear everything else. We fear the things we see about us, and the things we know from the stories and myths of our forefathers. Therefore we hold by our customs and observe all the rules of the tabu.[2]

---

2. Knud Rasmussen, *Across Arctic America* (The First Thule Expedition—Danish Ethnographical Expedition to Arctic North America, 1921-1924), 130-131.

Chapter One

Hunger

"Has the baby come?" the father called out.

"No," responded a weak voice from within a hurriedly-built ice shelter.

Alasurak paced the snow, scanning the far reaches for possible signs of life. Tilting his head slightly, he half listened for another sound coming from the hollow of the igloo.

"A girl," he thought.

Although the choice (if indeed one had a choice) offered no solution to their dilemma, he secretly

Alone in My Kayak

wished his wife would give them a daughter. A man usually preferred sons, for without hunters-to-be growing up among them, the future looked grim indeed. With an already larger than average family of five stair-step boys, Alasurak didn't feel that he needed another. As it was, their scant provisions hardly stretched to meet the demands of seven healthy appetites.

The husband stopped in his tracks. Had he heard something? He waited, but the snow hut cowered in silence. On with his musing. Everyone knew that a poorly-clad hunter was rarely successful. A man needed a woman skillful with the needle to tailor fine skin clothing. From that standpoint, girls could be considered an asset to their society in their role of protectively cladding the hunter. On the other hand, too many females were hard to keep. Put it this way: One does what he has to do.

Not exactly savoring these troubled thoughts, the father tried to rationalize the actions soon to follow. On the other hand, in their desperate situation, a girl who would likely eat less and later lift some of the mother's load might not be the worst. Perhaps they'd keep a sister for the boys at home.

Had this cutting edge of starvation threatened only Alasurak and Kignak, they might have turned

Hunger

to a neighbor for help. It was no use, though, for hunger wasn't playing favorites this time. An early winter moving in right on the heels of a skimpy summer back in 1891 had caught everyone off guard. That was not to imply that the dark months along the north coast of Alaska could ever be easy—but that particular lean time had to be the worst.

When their limited rations ran out, every able-bodied adult in their village set out on a disorganized sortie in search of food. They braved their way through snow that hung like smothering veil unfolded and swirling in the biting cold air. The hands of Arctic winds had stroked the drifts to form artistic yet somewhat monotonous patterns across the flat landscape. Often surface blended with sky to create a deceptive "white out," an eerie fantasy land.

On clear days a mountain chain stands silhouetted against the far horizon. These wild Alaskan Alps known as the Brooks Range demand respect. The venturer who loses direction among its maze of hills and valleys runs the risk of never finding his way out. Wild animals openly express their resentment toward intruders into a domain claimed by right of strength and cunning since time immemorial. Vengeful storms threaten to extinguish the breath of anyone who fails to find

Alone in My Kayak

shelter before they hit. That's the way it has been and that's the way it always will be.

Somewhere back in time, their forefathers had begun dotting the treeless coastline that was underscored with permafrost. A skilled hunter met his family's needs by harvesting seal, whale, walrus and other sea creatures. He scouted the waters in a streamlined kayak made of sealskin stretched tightly over a wooden frame. After slipping into the manhole with its stormsleeve cuff, he pulled a drawstring snugly around his waist so no water would seep in even if his canoe capsized. His harpoon and other equipment were secured on the outside and within easy reach. When hunting demanded teamwork, several men traveled together in an *umiak*, an open skin boat usually about 30 feet in length.

Migrating herds of caribou numbering tens of thousands crossed vast expanses of pristine lowlands in search of better feeding grounds. In summer myriads of pesky mosquitoes drove the animals to the beaches where a brisk breeze brought temporary relief from their needling tormentors. Caribou now graze only a few short miles from the sea in off seasons, but a century ago they kept a safe 50 to 100 miles inland. Therefore, when sea creatures grew scarce, hunters turned toward the hills.

Hunger

Back in that nearly-forgotten era before government subsidies, dozens of families faced extinction. Straggling groups of Eskimos abandoned their settlements, heading out in search of land animals. Having already used the last of their provisions, the people pushed against the elements with only one goal in mind: to find food.

Recycled snow erased the tracks made by the more able-bodied who broke trail; those who followed floundered through as best they could. Too tired to complain, they endured the discomfort of sweat and chill, of wet boots and aching feet. Their garments, designed for hard use, looked as tired as the wearers. A few men wore warm polar bear pants that clearly stated the wearer or a close family member excelled as an outstanding hunter. So what? Pride in being the provider had to take its beating too.

With hunger gnawing at their stomachs and pinching their nerves, the travelers kept their worn, *mukluks* (skin boots) moving leadenly over icy wastes. Their park ruffs designed to warm the air before it got to their lungs became heavy with frozen breath. Every movement was calculated to keep one warm, yet not to draw too heavily on one's remaining physical reserve. Depleted of its scant food supply, Alasurak's community was forced to eat some of the valuable sled dogs too.

Alone in My Kayak

The few dogs not yet sacrificed for food gnawed on worn-out harnesses and shreds of summer tents.

For the people, every bone had been picked clean and re-boiled to make a thin broth. Someone who was lucky enough to kill a lone bird painstakingly divided it. The hunter Alasurak got the tongue. What kind of a teaser do you call that? Chances were slim, but somewhere out there in blinding whiteness they might find tracks that would lead to food.

Although pregnant with their sixth child, Kignak had felt compelled to go with her husband. Like their neighbors, the couple trudged toward the foothills without seeing a trace of animal life. A hapless stray or remains of a caribou carcass left by the wolves would have been better than nothing. Hunger for them was bad enough, but what about their boys at home who no longer mustered enough energy to play outdoors?

Then the mother became weary—so weary that she could go no farther. The time had come for her to deliver.

Alasurak, a capable man with strong hands, hastily stacked snow blocks to make a birth house beside the Uttokkak River. Complying with an ancient custom that denied anyone being present when a child was born, he stepped outdoors when the hut was completed. Manhood also required that he act as if his wife and baby were of no deep concern to him. After a child had been given a proper name, however, a responsible father could hold his head high as he carried out his role of protector and provider.

For the present, Alasurak guarded his emotions by concentrating on dark spots he detected in the distance. Caribou? Maybe his overworked imagination. It wasn't easy to tell in pale daylight robbed of the sun's direct rays. Two months yet before its return....

In spite of the pressures that kept Alasurak out of the windowless igloo, his thoughts went to her who was bringing his child into the world. She bore labor pains, he the guilt. If only he could help his wife at a time like this.

No, for he had to preserve his dignity. Everyone knew that a man's occupation outranked that of a woman's—she whose allotted tasks were mostly sewing, cooking and tanning hides. Nor did their women often complain, at least not with treats. Little wonder that northern races learned both to endure and to reflect hardness—a natural result of generations fighting for existence in a bleak land. Man against animal, man against nature. Always against. To fight, to oppose, to struggle. That seemed to be what life was all about. Even though culture might endorse misplaced priorities, it failed to relieve an accompanying sense of blame. Alasurak, a caring husband and father, would have done better by a whelping husky.

A sound from within the windbreak broke his thoughts. He breathed a sigh of relief. At least that was over with! And Kignak was still living. Putting up a front of indifference, the father called out in the harsh voice expected of him, "Has the baby come yet?"

Through the small entrance he heard a wavering, "Yes."

"What kind? Boy or girl?"

"Boy."

"Boy? Put him in the snow then. Let him die. We have no food for him. Best to put him in the snow."

The man waited. Surely Kignak had heard what he said. "Better for him to die, better than to be hungry," he shouted.

No answer.

Alasurak could feel his temper rising, but he restrained himself. Why direct his anger at his woman? It made more sense to vent his frustration

Hunger

on whatever the forces were that drove a man to such a choice as this.

"Hear me, Kignak? Put him in the snow!"

His wife knew as well as he did that they already had too many children. She should talk back and they'd argue it out, but a silence that demanded hearing declared her intention all too clearly. No force on earth could make her give up this parcel of humanity she had carried close to her heart for months. Lay him out to the mercy—which was no mercy—of winter? Never!

Alasurak's strength of character didn't turn him over to a blind rage. Sure, he could assert authority, let his wife know who was boss. He also knew that he was ahead in the long run. At least his wife wasn't one of those women who yap like nervous pups. That's the kind that wears a fellow down.

Thus, without a battle the mother emerged the winner and the parents who couldn't rejoice over the birth of another child dragged the unmeasured miles back home.

Were they being downright stupid, coming with this helpless being when they hadn't been able to feed the five they already had? The boys expecting food would see instead a scrawny crying baby. One more mouth.

Alone in My Kayak

Once again within the confines of their own walls, Kignak held her baby close to her emaciated breasts. The infant's tongue tried to suckle. His clenched fists struck out in protest, but she who had given him life had nothing with which to sustain it. Like everyone else, the mother suffered from lack of proper nourishment. His brothers didn't bother to watch. Nothing about the scene sparked their interest or coaxed even the faintest smile to their lips.

At last admitting that she was unable to nurse her baby or to otherwise satisfy his demands, Kignak reversed her decision. No longer could she bear listening to his feeble cries. She had said she would never do it, but she had to....

With a brave front she wrapped her baby's fur bunting tightly around him before placing him in a soft mound of snow close to a traveled route. Putting him farther out on the terrain might negate a hope that somehow someone would find him. If someone walked by, someone who could pick him up and care for him...

Woman, woman, put away idle thoughts. You know that this winter everyone in your village and in the whole world hungers.

What else could she do? Kignak saw herself without an option. That she had refused this last

Hunger

resort only a day or two before did nothing to salve her hurt. What had she accomplished by her valiant effort to save his life, other than prolong suffering? Perhaps she could ease her pain by reminding herself of the generations of women before her who had done the same. They understood that babies go quickly. Nature provided for that too.

With heart and mind battling one against the other, the mother turned stoically away. If the couple hurried, they might catch up with the others who were by now a few miles closer to the mountains.

Chapter Two

Fear

Life could be pleasant enough when the Eskimos had plenty of whale and seal meat. When the pot filled with caribou soup steamed over the open fire, smiling oiled faces shone in the sputtering light of the stone lamp. It was another story when land and sea failed to yield their expected returns and supplies ran perilously low.

Fear nagged at the polar peoples all the way across Siberia, North America and Greenland as well as the scattered townships of northern Scandinavia and Lapland that also felt the mean pinch of endlessly trying to cope. With no warm Gulf

Stream to encourage vegetation along their coasts, the battle for life among the Eskimos quite literally became a bloody fight.

These semi-nomadic family groups escaped extinction by continually adjusting to freak turns of weather and contending with the rawest aspects of the wild. For the most part, it was their specialization in hunting techniques that gave them the toehold needed to pull through. But for all their ingenuity, the Inuit calculated almost no appreciable population increase over the centuries. The hardiest made it by tricking (if possible) the merciless hand of fate—whatever that might be. If worse came to worst, the size of one's family might have to be purposely reduced. These primitive forms of bargaining with nature, however, only added to their forebodings.

"Whose fault is it?" The question that tried to shift blame elsewhere couldn't always find its answer in another person. So, in spite of the various disputes common to any society, a commitment to animism provided something of an escape route. The people chose to believe that lurking behind whatever took place were unseen powers that ruled over weather, birds, fish and animals—people too. This form of religion reasoned that everything, whether animate or inanimate, embraced a spirit—an *inua* representing a controlling force. Because these spirits were a menacing lot—rarely did anything please them—one must always be on the lookout. They'd twist your best intentions to use them against you. *See there? It comes as predicted—depression, sickness, storms. The spirits—who displeased them? Who or what's to blame?*

Whose fault? Angry spirits could also serve as a convenient out for the person wanting to escape undue criticism. *Inuas* in the lower echelons were awarded some excuse too for, conniving as they were, they also had to bow to a reputed chain of command. All of this came from the moon's spirit, who supposedly reigned supreme. From his exalted position this sinister being observed earth's inhabitants, carefully noting and tallying every move. If his subjects wittingly or otherwise challenged his absolute authority, he hid his face behind dark storm clouds to pout. But look out if his displeasure went deep enough for him to turn the elements loose over a helpless cluster of people! When revenge comprised the very core of his disposition, death followed. Or so the whispered tales went.

Apprehensions—there was no escaping them. Nevertheless these served as a wretched kind of adhesion that held the populace together as they agreed on regulations that might keep them on the safe side of a common foe. Accompanying taboos and superstitions passed down from one generation to the next were added "just in case." Enough of these rules crisscrossing each other might eventually constitute some kind of protective wall against that which they dreaded most: famine. If not upon them at the moment, it lurked just around the corner.

Thus, needing to stay on good terms with the creatures he took for food, the least a hunter could do was offer gestures of respect to these animal spirits. After killing a caribou, he hoped for further good luck by slipping his thank-you note (whatever token he found handy) under a stone. Before skinning the seal he caught, he might put melted snow in its mouth to quench its thirst. These touches of kindness that helped preserve a creature's dignity might persuade them to let themselves be taken again.

The men, however, didn't carry the entire weight of these rituals and taboos. Women also were expected to complete certain tasks before a hunt began, for if they worked at home-centered projects while the men went out after game, the animal's *inua* might be insulted. Then it could retaliate by pressuring the offenders emotionally, inducing fainting spells. A woman expecting a child took the full brunt of appeasing its whims.

So it was that, at a time when she most needed someone standing by, she entered the birthing house alone. After she delivered, she returned to her home physically and mentally exhausted.

If new life endangered a dwelling, how much more devilment accompanied a death? When someone died, the family quickly removed the body through a hole in the roof—outwitting the spirit lest it return to harass them. A hunter was usually placed in a shallow grave along with tools and other items he might be needing for his journey into the unknown. Women were buried with a few household items and sewing things. If a mother died in childbirth, the living infant might also be laid to rest with her.

These and countless other rituals the moonman supposedly watched over anxiously. Laws broken in some abstract way contributed to the disorder of his house with the sum total becoming an abomination to him. Then oh! fiendish delight! The ogre found his reason for wielding hunger's sword. Since by now only *angakok* (a shaman or witch doctor) could bring about a reconciliation, he must take a long journey to the outer world to tidy up the moonman's dwelling. Once that haughty ruler of the skies had been appeased, he might withdraw his curse.

Alone in My Kayak

The shaman carefully set the stage for his space trip, a ceremony apparently most effective when performed in the presence of as many onlookers as possible. After extinguishing the crude stone lamp, he lay bound on the floor in total darkness. Then, to the accompaniment of monotonous incantations and the incessant beating of skin drums, he made his exit. Mesmerized by sound, bystanders in fascinated horror tried to grasp what the physically helpless man was saying. His talk becoming totally unintelligible served as a sign that his soul had finally made contact with the highest echelon.

With no one knowing for sure what was going on, mysticism played its full role. Re-entering earth's sphere, the people's go-between assured those present that his mission had indeed accomplished its purpose. He who ruled over night skies would release the animals, bidding them to return to their accustomed habitats. The people would again live in plenty. If hunting suddenly picked up, the shaman was duly honored for his persuasive powers. His words carried weight and he ate well.

What if his luck failed? He could try something else. Seldom were his abilities questioned, for no one wanted an enemy capable of invoking more evil. Generally speaking, shamans were first-rate con artists, although there were undoubtedly those who tried to serve their people in the only way they knew how. Life wasn't all easy, either, for a man whose negative role often ruled him out of desirable friendships. What young person felt like seeking out a shaman for warm fatherly advice? Also, if he believed even a fraction of what he himself predicted, certainly the fears a witch doctor dispensed would return to haunt him. His was a kind of unending job too, always trying to keep peace with the nether world.

Whispered rumors told about lesser spirits as well, the impossible-to-please *qivitit*. These contemptible ones preferred the trackless tundra and foothills of distant mountains. Unlike ordinary *inuas*, they were reputed to be people who got lost or who had purposely disappeared to join unseen forces, becoming a kind of half-human, half-spirit specie. This supposed alliance with demonic beings troubled the travelers, plaguing their long journeys with nagging premonitions. Fear laid the base for fancied encounters when behind every rock or snow mound lurked a possible threat to their safety. They might even run into one of the troublesome "little people," counterparts of the trolls from old Norse tales. Of course no one could prove the existence of these stunted beings, although folks claimed to have seen them. Hearsay compounded their deeds, blaming them for stealing food supplies or driving away a man's dog team and leaving him to freeze alone. Never were these mini-devils up to any good.

With this assortment of diabolical forces working against the human race, how could one be sure that the shaman's power was adequate? Even if it was, a man alone out on the tundra could run into an emergency. It was best to play it safe with each person finding for himself a magic formula as a safeguard. He'd have his own personal "rabbit's foot," an amulet that he carried in his pocket or sewed into the seam of one of his garments. The luckiest charms generally came from an animal, thus inviting the creature's spirit to lend its particular cunning or prowess. A bear tooth could ensure strength, a fox claw swift action. Yet, for all these painstaking precautions, there was no absolute guarantee against the forces of evil. Animism became an endless quest for something more powerful with which to combat them, but the more one regarded his ancestors' superstitions, the heavier his oppression.

The endlessness of winter white didn't help either; uncharted expanses hold a powerful element of suggestion for people of any race. There was more than one rhyme of an ancient mariner back when they sailed by the stars or at best by a

Fear

primitive compass. Water, water everywhere, and too much time to think.

Snow as far as the eye could see had somewhat the same effect. If only the uneasy traveler could see something to break the monotony.... With that on his mind, who knows what apparition might suddenly appear?

Chapter Three

Deliverance

Moving in early, the winter of 1891 carried a strange foreboding. It seemed as if every contrary force in the north reached out to join hands in a pact to make life intolerable for the Inuit. Shamans who hadn't succeeded in appeasing the unsmiling moonman went hungry with everybody else. Day after day hunters had gone out on the ice to check breathing holes, but not a solitary seal showed its nose. Fish? Gone. A defeated handful of people saw no alternative but to continue their trek toward the mountains in quest of anything that resembled food.

Alone in My Kayak

An old woman crawled out of a tiny igloo and stumbled along some distance behind the others. No one paid much attention to one whose years were soon to be up anyway. Walking slowly, shoulders stooped and head lowered, the grandmother noticed a bundle. A cocoon. Ah, how well she knew....

The woman paused, realizing it should have been she lying out alone somewhere. An unwritten law, well established by precedent, decreed that in famine the elderly be given up to die. The community must make room for youth, for those who would perpetuate the race. Not infrequently these older ones were placed far out on the ice where a chunk easily broken off drifts conveniently away to open sea. Or the old and ill were simply left behind when it came time for the family to relocate. So be it. You can't stand in line for years and suddenly object because it's your turn to go.

All things considered, the old one had nothing to lose if she chose to add to the burden of her own tired bones. Silently she reached for the baby. After brushing the powdery snow from his bunting, she lifted the edge of her soiled parka as with practiced hand she slipped him underneath. Bending over farther, she jostled the infant until he rested on the hump of her shoulders. Were she younger, he could have nestled better in the contour of her upper back, but years of toil had changed that.

Though she had no belt to tie around her waist, her stoop was enough to hold him. Neither would he smother, for the fur lining of her parka allowed for ample air. Barely able to make out the sketchy footprints ahead of her, the grandmother shuffled on. A numbing cold crept into her joints. Her *mukluks* dragged through the snow. What's that her mind said? Lift her feet? Her muscles refusing to accept the command, she sank to the ground, lacking the strength to push herself up again. Maybe she had found her final resting place.

No one saw the woman drop, but later a hunter watchful for any kind of movement turned aside and stopped. He sensed life. "*Inuk* (person). Is someone here?"

A faint, muffled whimper that carried through the Arctic stillness confirmed his hunches. Strong hands reached through the drifts for a small person, but it seemed as if the child was part of something else. To lift one meant lifting two. How long the old woman had been lying there before the man found her, no one knew. For that matter no one knew that she was old except by comparison. In those days the measures taken to stay alive swung back to cut short one's life span.

Why couldn't she be left to die? Endless sleep beckoned. Then she remembered. Although nearly paralyzed by exhaustion, the infant's self-appointed guardian accepted the support that put her on her feet again. Reaching back she felt for the bundle. Still there. With that her protesting limbs obeyed her determined will, for she had more than herself to think about now. Strange that she should feel a stirring of hope at such a time as this....

Before the afternoon gray merged into black night, the families who had fanned out to better scrutinize a sizeable area for game regrouped to make cavelike shelters from chunks of packed snow. There in a dull absence of neighborly talk they lay down to rest. Nothing new to think about, nothing new to say. Rubbing their hands to induce circulation into numbed fingers, the travelers drew closer together for warmth as they shared relief from the chilling winds that had buffeted them all day long. The only child among them, a tiny baby, lay close against his rescuer. His weak cries would waken no one but her—and perhaps other mothers with little ones left behind....

Thick walls of their igloos muffled any sounds from without. With no cross ventilation, the air became so heavy that they slept as if drugged. Sleep and forget the string of yesterdays that famine had

Deliverance

blurred into one long siege. Tomorrow offered only futility, continued hours of whip-cracking hunger driving them on to nowhere in particular.

The dawn of another day. Strange that none of the travelers had been disturbed by the sound of hoofs breaking through the crusted snow. A herd of caribou had come to feed just outside the snow huts where the people slept! The animals pawed and scraped, uncovering moss and lichens that clung to the rocks. After munching an early breakfast, they lay down to rest before going on their way again.

It's not unlikely that the first hunter to get a glimpse of the pastoral scene thought he was dreaming. Maybe it was a tantalizing prelude to death, a mirage of sorts. If it was real, he must share it.

"You see it?"

"Yes. Wake up the others."

Hurried whispers. Surely everyone couldn't be imagining the same thing!

Within seconds skilled hunters reached for their spears and crawled through the doorway. Beside themselves with an exotic mixture of joy and fear, the women reached for clubs, walking sticks or whatever else they also might use to kill. As soon as the first few animals were downed, the men tore at the raw meat, cramming it into their mouths. Eating ravishingly, they gained strength to engage in mad pursuit of the fleeing herd.

Intoxicated with the warm blood they had greedily slurped, hunters plunged into a frenzied slaughter, yelling commands at the women who had already begun hacking and butchering in primitive style. Perhaps in the melee someone tried to send right thoughts to whatever power had rescued them in this last desperate hour. Whatever power? Certainly not the moonman, for such unheard-of benevolence didn't become him.

Despite most of the calves being big enough to fend for themselves, among the caribou was a cow that still had milk. One determined grandmother turned dairywoman. As quickly as her gnarled fingers would let her, she stripped out a couple of ounces of the warm milk. If her baby's stomach didn't reject this bit of nourishment, he had a chance to make up for his slow start in life. The old woman waited. Exactly what she had counted on! He kept the milk down and worked his lips as if asking for more.

Grandmother chuckled. She knew what she'd do when the workers threw themselves down for a rest. After gumming a sliver of meat to a soft pulp,

Deliverance

she shoved a tiny bit into the baby's mouth. Not that she expected him to swallow it, but they needed this lighthearted break. To the delight of the onlookers, he smacked his lips before his little tongue forced the wad from his mouth.

"Ah, this child," she clucked to herself, stroking his cheek with the back of her hand. Was he a favorable sign, a harbinger like the first snowbird of spring heralding better days ahead?

Hunger pangs satisfied, the travelers tingled with new vitality oozing into every fiber of their beings. When other Eskimos joined their group, younger recruits set out to track down more caribou. At last, with provisions such as they hadn't seen in months, they felt that they could return to their nearly-abandoned village. Most of the dogs had already been sacrificed for food; only a couple of owners had been able to hold the age-old rule that a few huskies be kept no matter what. Weak as they were, these would be pressed into service alongside manpower.

"Here, help strap this to my back," someone shouted as he struggled with a makeshift carrier. Others, in lieu of dogs, formed human teams to drag carcasses back to their settlement. Think of it! Food for weeks to come!

Enthusiasm soared to an all-time high as both men and women pitched in to do more than their

Alone in My Kayak

allotted share before afternoon shadows absorbed their few hours of daylight. A nucleus of hunters volunteered to stay at the site to guard the surplus from the wolves that always followed a herd. For in spite of inbred urges to kill, a pack of wolves will turn aside to steal once they have picked up the scent of fresh blood.

The oldest and the youngest among the group rated the honor of being among the first to ride back to the village atop a creaking, groaning sled. In one of the village's sod igloos, five thin hollow-eyed boys waited, but for what they weren't sure. While some sat staring into nothingness, others napped. Suddenly one of them stirred. Did you hear that? A sled! They listened more closely, for the runners on a weighted sled make their own peculiar crunch as they break through the snow. Besides, the dogs barked as if they were expecting a full reward for their efforts. Just maybe....

Crawling up and out of the igloo in leaden response to the musher's shout, they blinked their eyes in astonishment. There sat Grandmother, their grandmother, waving a mittened hand, all the wrinkles in her face smiling. And meat, *meat*, MEAT! Then another surprise as she carefully unwrapped a familiar fur bundle to show them the baby brother they hadn't thought about seeing again. Mother and father, whom the children

Deliverance

called Aaka and Aapa, would be coming soon too. They would be all together—plus one—again.

This, the story he grew up hearing, Patkotak liked to retell. "And so," he closed with a certain flourish, "back in November, 1891, I came into the poor sod hut as the sixth son in a row of sons."

That evening the happy parents did more than tend the lamp. Aapa added driftwood to the burning fat in their rock pit in the center of the room. Afterwards he went out to remove the frame holding their opaque skylight in place. This window, probably no more than two feet square with a pane of tightly stretched *oogruk* (bearded seal) stomach allowed a faint suggestion of light to filter in. Alasurak had to lift it off to let the smoke escape and create a draft for the fire. After eating enough raw meat to satiate their appetites, they lay thick slices of caribou meat on the hot stones to roast. Later they could cook larger chunks in a stone pot, or in an iron pot left by early whalers. In spite of preparing their food without the advantage of seasoning, no one asked for better. They ate with the finest of all condiments—appreciation.

Chapter Four

Learning

Alaskurak's boys grew up in an Alaska-type igloo, a sod hut reinforced with whale bone and driftwood. Built partially underground, the solid structure with thick earthen walls provided excellent insulation. A low doorway marked the entrance which led down into the storage area; that in turn opened into the house proper, a room measuring about 12 feet square. Its one small window skimped on light and fresh air; a larger opening might invite polar bears that got a whiff of seal oil or meat roasting over the fire—the pleasant odors.

Alone in My Kayak

Poor ventilation served to trap the damp smelly air caused by a lot of living in limited space. An open container holding the urine used in tanning hides aggravated the family's lack of sanitary facilities. Aaka, who did her sewing indoors during the winter months, needed the skins for boots and parkas, bedding and tents. She also made their thread by carefully splitting lengths of caribou sinew with her teeth. Such close living contributed heavily to tuberculosis, which took a high toll among the native peoples. Nor did the scourge confine itself to only those races, for other northern people likewise recognized the symptoms of a disease the Scandinavians identified as "quick consumption."

Tight quarters became even more cramped on stormy days when children crowded indoors. Boys learned to carve on bits of driftwood or leftover scraps of ivory, making playthings like yo-yos and darts. Later they would use their own handmade slings to bring down birds in flight. Girls practiced skin sewing and helped with the cooking. Time didn't drag for imaginative youngsters accustomed to making up their own games, unless winter storms kept them cooped up for days on end.

A woman from one of the coastal villages described those dismal intervals during her

Learning

childhood: "I still fight waves of loneliness when the wind moans and whistles around the corner of my house. Though I now have TV and my family to keep me company, those days when we had nothing to do come back to me. We children could only amuse ourselves so long. Then we would band together for protection against the storm.

"Running from house to house, we shoved our way in to look for something interesting going on. Usually nothing exciting. We stood in a huddle by the door, watched a while, then ran to the next place. If only we had books or paper and pencils. The nothingness was hard to handle. So for me," she added with a slight shudder as if to shake off memories, "storms will always spell loneliness."

With a break in weather, the reflection from the glistening snow helped dispel winter's darkness. The youngsters were playing outdoors again and, like boys and girls everywhere, they laughed and cried, they fought for fun and fought to settle scores. All the while learning.

Once the boys picked up the knack of throwing bolas (two or more pieces of heavy bone attached to strings of sinew), they killed birds in flight by entangling their feet and wings, which hurled them to the ground. This silent method of hunting proved especially effective for getting eider ducks that flew over the tundra.

Alone in My Kayak

Little fellows practiced the art of kayak paddling, even on land. Along beaches covered with stones smooth from millennia of being rolled by waves and honed by icebergs, they found material for building dreams. Sitting between two rows of sizeable rocks, these future hunters fancied themselves in real kayaks. A piece of driftwood became a paddle, a slender branch from distant shores a fine harpoon.

Most of them, of course, had only a vague concept of the real work involved in keeping ahead of the hunger threat that nagged their elders. They were used to seeing a hunter leave with a couple of large nets over one shoulder and a long, hooked wooden pole resting on the other. In his hands he carried an ice chisel and a dipper. A long way out on the frozen sea where the ice was many feet thick, he stopped. If unable to find a natural crack in the ice, he painstakingly cut through it. By checking the currents he determined the probability of seals coming there before partially concealing the opening with snow, leaving only a small breathing hole.

The following evening the hunter returned to see if seals had used his vent. If they had, he quickly chiseled another, larger hole several feet away from it. After tying together his two nets (each about 12 feet square), he let them down with his

Learning

long-handled tool. The nets hung loosely between the openings, stone weights keeping them from floating upward or drifting with the current. Additional weights helped secure them to the surface ice.

With his trap completed, the hunter planted a stick in the soft snow right at the edge of his nets and waited. A toppled stick meant a seal was caught. All he had to do was pull the seal through the larger opening.

As fathers and big brothers told their stories, the youngsters with their mind's eye could see the hunter at sea paddling without sound. Imagination ran wild as the boys fancied themselves doing the same, tingling with desire for their turn to surprise an unsuspecting prey. They'd have to wait a few more years, however, before putting their growing store of knowledge to practical use. Until then, they had to tag along with the womenfolk until one of them spotted a kayak edging toward the shore.

"Aapa's coming, Aapa's coming. He's got something big!" he yelled.

Like a shot the youngsters turned, running toward the water's edge. All they needed to see was a man's shoulders above the ice floes. The effort bent to his strokes as he paddled along told them right away the size of his game.

When the hunter pulled up to the beach, his wife or another woman took over immediately. Quick with their pie-shaped *ulus* (women's knives), these talented skinners could flay a seal in less than three minutes. A long slash from throat to back fin lay the animal open while shorter strokes cutting into layers of fat removed the hide. Several animals brought in at once triggered lighthearted rivalry.

"I'll beat you!" With that the game was on, racing to see who could skin a seal first without nicking the valuable hide. (You can't have holes in your boots before they're made.) The first one done straightened her shoulders as with the back of her bloodied hands she laughingly pushed aside strands of hair that had fallen across her face. Small children formed a stubby wall that wiggled annoyingly close to the workers, begging for first rights to the liver or some other choice part of the seal.

Eating raw meat didn't always invite trouble, but the chances were nonetheless there—especially with polar bear meat. Biologists maintain that trichinosis brought on by eating raw meat came first from the sea. As a result, entire families died from poisoning. The Arctic peoples most likely acquired their taste for frozen fish and game out of necessity. Hunting far out on the ice with no fuel

Learning

on hand, tired men filled their stomachs with whatever they could get. They had to eat for strength to go on, or drop from exhaustion before making it home.

Teenagers often accompanied their parents when they searched for food during the winter. Dressed in the warmest furs, they stood motionless with harpoon in hand waiting for a seal that would sooner or later swim to a breathing hole. When an unsuspecting animal finally stuck its nose up for a breath of fresh air, it became their target.

According to legend, someone once suggested taking along an oil lamp to help them keep warm. It was short comfort. In the flurry of spotting a seal, the lamp got knocked over and several of the hunters were severely burned when their parkas caught on fire. It served as a reminder that it paid to stick to proven methods.

If seal meat was the Eskimo's bread and butter, a successful whale hunt equaled a herd of cattle on the hoof. Such a hunt was another ball game entirely, one that called for the ultimate in teamwork even though, for the most part, their culture hadn't produced strong leaders. Chiefs and kings were practically unknown in a culture where, most of the time, men paddled their kayaks alone and families learned to fend for themselves. This individualistic background offered its own rewards, however, allowing a man personal pride in providing for those dependent upon him. So what better life than to live near the sea where one can reap of its rich harvest!

These pleasures notwithstanding, the scheming ocean had its own way of demanding a dear price for what it gave. Father, son or brother might not come home at the end of the day. Until their fate was known for sure, a bonfire on the beach served as a beacon for the one who might be lost. Only quick, well-calculated moves enabled a man to get away from an ill-tempered walrus that with one hack of his strong tusks could split a kayak in two.

Turnabout is fair play. The walrus could also end up the loser if his pursuer kept a cool head and used his weapon to full advantage. Anyone returning with such a trophy unquestionably deserved the prestige it gave him.

More often an organized hunt involving several men in an *umiak* brought home that prize. Besides providing more meat than a seal, walrus generally won the vote as being tastier. The flippers, fermented to add tang to an otherwise bland diet, rated as a specialty.

Traders eagerly bought the ivory tusks whenever they could. Not all, though, for the carvers

Learning

wisely kept some for their own use. Long winter evenings invited them to work with their hands as they listened to legends from their past and stories packed with sound advice for the up-coming generation.

A narrator might dare to embellish here or there, especially if he sensed his listeners' attention being diverted. Among his own people he wouldn't get away with stretching the truth. A stranger, however, might have a hard time determining what actually took place if the speaker wanted a bit of fun. But for all that, these self-styled historians played an important role as reference librarians in both folklore and earth science.

There was something cozy too about huddling together in close quarters while the wind circled the outer walls. Stories of bygone days took on an eerie touch when shadows moved and stretched themselves grotesquely out of proportion against inside walls. The children wrapped themselves tighter in their fur covers, ears out.

"Go to sleep," Aaka ordered, knowing that of course they wouldn't. Her mother had said the same to her. What if some of the tales sent shivers up your spine? That was all the more reason to snuggle closer to your brother while straining for tidbits that put a person really in the know.

Alone in My Kayak

The boys needed to absorb all they could. In their futures waited the means of the livelihood their fathers knew. As soon as a toddler was allowed out on his own, he played dog sled. By the time he was five years old he became the proud owner of a scaled-to-size sled and a puppy to train. Then, before either dog or master filled out another winter, they aimed at being leaders.

"Eee-oh! Eee-oh!" shouted these beginners as they competed on short runs. Smaller children followed, shrieking their delight. Keeping at it, a boy could learn within a few weeks how to run alongside a sled with one hand holding the "uprights." With his dog pulling at top speed, the young musher threw himself into the sled, thus sharpening the reflexes so important for making time on the trail. What a sense of authority when he shouted commands at his obedient dog—the ideal, of course. In reality the practice included many tumbling-in-the-snow experiences for both of them.

When the heads of families went out on the ice with their teams, these future mushers often followed a short way out of the village. They knew the boundaries, however. Not only was it forbidden to push beyond clearly defined limits, but dangerous. A fellow had to qualify in size and strength before daring a tour over ocean ice.

Learning

Alasurak wouldn't hear of his youngest son tagging along on a real hunt, but Patkotak could dream anyway—dream big. Then came the moment of temptation. He had to prove that being the youngest didn't mean he was a baby. Even if no one else praised him, he would know himself what he had done. With his dog Quimmeq and his very own sled, he'd follow a mite farther than the usual "part way" deemed safe.

Patkotak cautiously held back, far enough to hide his true intentions. Quimmeq loped along at an uneven pace, lining the tracks of the full-sized sled with prints of his own.

The village had slipped out of sight when overconfident Patkotak began having doubts. He'd better go back. Pushing and pulling, he and Quimmeq turned the sled around. Go back? A fine white powder drifting gently down from gray skies had subtly wiped out the tracks he had counted on to lead him home. Never mind, in some way they'd find out how to retrace their route. To his dismay, the young musher soon realized that landmarks weren't easily identified without a sod hut in sight. Winter had tricked him, blotting out every familiar rock, smoothing over the few ground formations he might have recognized.

The snow began to fall heavier, blurring the boy's vision until he could scarcely see a few yards

Alone in My Kayak

ahead. Bothersome tears! He brushed them away hastily. No, he told himself, he wasn't crying—the cold made his eyes and nose run. His sleeve could take care of that.

Despite having lost all sense of direction, the little fellow helped his dog by running alongside and breaking through small drifts. Then he became so tired that he got into the sled, leaving it to his comrade to decide which way to go. Quimmeq, hardly more than a pup, didn't know the way either.

Patkotak got out again to do the master's share when a gust of wind slapped him down. He struggled to his feet, but his fingers, numb with cold, didn't want to take a firm grip on anything. After several futile attempts, he gave up. Falling back into the sled, he gave vent to the hulking sobs he had held back too long.

Never had he been this lonesome and alone in the world. Now the worst wasn't that Aapa would be unhappy with him; the worst was that maybe he would never see Aapa again. Or Aaka either. As if understanding these fears, Quimmeq padded softly over to his master and licked his face.

Patkotak repented. If only he had stayed home! What if no one ever found him? He would die alone in the snow, like his mother said had almost happened when he was a baby. Aaka believed that God in Heaven had spared his life by sending

Learning

Grandmother along to pick him up. What she said, he chose to accept.

Guilt nibbled at his conscience. He alone was to blame, so what were his chances? Childlike faith asserted itself. He would ask God anyway to once more send someone along to find him. He couldn't call on the other spirits because he was afraid of them. Besides, it was probably because of them that he nearly died right after he was born. That he was sure of because the older people said so.

The child couldn't handle anymore. He had no idea how to word a prayer, but his heart and mind cried, "Send someone who knows the way home."

Exhausted, his thoughts drifted.... Quimmeq too would have given in to the comfort of puppy sleep had instinct not told him that something was wrong with his young master. It was up to him to keep watch. Curled into a ball, he closed his eyes as if napping while keeping his sharp ears open.

It had been a good day for Aapa who was headed home with a sledful of caribou. Although a heavy load kept him from breaking trail very fast, he mushed confidently ahead. It had stopped snowing and he had lots of time.

Suddenly he had an idea. He'd swing out over the ice and get a seal while luck was still with him.

Alone in My Kayak

Fresh oil to complement the lean caribou meat! Alasurak carried the reputation of being an exceptional hunter who could travel days without becoming fatigued as long as he had some *muktuk* (fibrous fatty tissue between the skin and underlying fat of the whale) to chew on. In top condition also, his well-fed dogs still strained in the harness to get through the new snow. With strong leisurely movements, Alasurak gave the sled an occasional shove to help them along.

Hey, there! What goes? Without warning, his team lurched and tugged at the tow line, gaining momentum with each bound just as they did when nearing a village. Some of them lifted their heads and howled as if responding to other dogs in chorus. Knowing his was the only team out that day, Alasurak was puzzled. There could be no other dogs this far from home. Holding on tightly to the sled, he had to exert every ounce of his strength to keep up with their uneven, excited pace. Even though the hunter hadn't heard anything, there might be a stray somewhere out in the drifts. Still, he couldn't stop long enough to be sure. Then he heard it, a lone cry that took on the same eager tones his own dogs had expressed moments before.

At a glance the man got the full picture. A short distance from the well-traveled route, he found

Learning

Patkotak's sled. Wagging his tail, the loyal pup still in harness danced excitedly.

The boy. Was he all right? Carefully his father reached out to awaken him. Startled, Patkotak fought to rub sleep from his eyes. Then, remembering what he had done, he began to cry. Between sobs he spilled out the whole story, promising never again to leave home by himself. Tenderly wrapping his son in his own sled bag to break the wind, Aapa placed him on top of his load. Loved and forgiven, the boy smiled contentedly. Well-trained huskies pulled toward home with Quimmeq running happy circles beside them.

In the meantime, home itself stirred with activity. The youngest had been gone for hours and no one had seen him leave. Obviously he had lost his way when it began to snow, but what direction might he have taken? Perhaps he had gone toward the sea. Sledding as far as it seemed possible for him to have gone, his brothers looked and called. They found no clue to Patkotak's whereabouts.

After a fruitless search the boys gave up and reluctantly headed back. Nearing the village, they heard the dogs—sure indication Aapa had returned. The brothers exchanged furtive glances. They could hardly wait to see what their father had gotten, but what would he say when he learned about little brother's absence?

"Look!" one of the boys shouted. "There he is!"

"Who?"

"Patkotak. Jumping down off the big sled!"

Sure enough. There was short-legged Patkotak running toward their snow-covered hut with Quimmeq at his heels, and Aaka and Aapa beaming in the background.

While fresh caribou simmered over a low fire, the family talked over the day's events, each including his part in the search for the lost one. They drew closer to eat while the youngest, gnawing at a bone, sat alone on the edge of his caribou skin. He didn't want to talk—they all knew his story anyway. Besides, it wasn't like that first time when he was rescued and he came out in a nice big way, almost like a hero. The painful truth of this episode had stripped his pride. Leave a guy alone and let him lick his wounds.

Drowsiness like a soft covering of new snow settled over one very tired boy as the bone slipped from his grasp. Patkotak was sound asleep.

Chapter Five

Transition

The nineteenth-century industrial revolution threw the western world into an upheaval, shifting population masses from rural to urban. At the same time pioneers of varying intent introduced new, often conflicting, sets of values to the north. The natives were being forced to make decisions on an unfamiliar plane.

In the old days, when hunters came home with only a few seals, no one asked, "What's for supper?" They ate what they had. Homemakers confined to basics worked with the sewing materials on hand—fur or skin with accents of ivory. Centuries-old patterns bore repeating until the day that speck on the horizon turned out to be a ship coming their way. It was many times the size of their biggest *umiak* and the trader aboard displayed a tantalizing assortment of merchandise. Never had they seen the like!

The hunter feasted his eyes before deciding what he wanted most. Tobacco or tea? Rice or a new hammer? A color-hungry woman fingered bolts of bright prints. Should she settle for blue dots or flowers with splashes of red? Or perhaps plain soft washable flannel for her baby?

"Make up your mind!"

Only it took more than a snap of the finger. Tastes and desires lying dormant for centuries couldn't surface that easily. While some of the people took immediate advantage of these new offers, others smarted with bitter frustration. The sands of sameness which had spelled security were fast slipping away from under their toes. They could easily loose their footing.

Bent on getting the most for their money, many of the *tanniks* (white leader people) hit the coast with a tempting supply of alcohol. Sin and disease tagged at its heels. Among these traders, however, were noteworthy exceptions. The older women of Point Hope smiled as they recalled the good will of

Transition

one kindly sea captain. Knowing about hungry winters, he came with sacks of flour to trade for furs and ivory. If only he had initiated the bartering with a stack of pancakes and a bottle of maple syrup!

"We felt sneaky about what we did," one of the women later confessed. "We were sure that white stuff was good for something, but we didn't know what. So we waited until his ship had sailed far enough away that the captain couldn't see us. Then we hurried to cut threads and open sacks. We dotted the beach with hundred-pound heaps of flour, and laughed when the wind blew the white powder back onto us. It was funny!

"That happened a long time ago when flour came in printed sacks. We could hardly wait—rushing home to sew, to make things with our pretty cloth. Now we know it was wasteful to throw away flour, but back then we didn't understand."

Seamen talked of coming back to stay, but someone else came first, the year before Patkotak was born. Two Presbyterian churchmen were aboard the Coast Guard cutter *Bear* as it made its annual run to the "top of the world": Sheldon Jackson, the missionary whose one-man campaign moved Congress to establish an educational system in Alaska, and Professor Leander Stevenson, a

Alone in My Kayak

45-year-old teacher from Ohio. It was an honor just to step on board the vessel known as "the mercy ship," so called because it freighted supplies to the government rescue station at Barrow. On this run it did the north one of its greatest favors for, although Jackson had a round trip in mind, Stevenson had booked one way.

Stevenson set foot on a sandy point outside the village of less then 200 Inuit to become the first missionary-teacher on the Arctic slope. He couldn't have had any idea what he was getting into, filling the multiple roles of doctor, nurse, teacher and counselor. When he could break away from caring for his neighbors' needs, he scrounged for driftwood, looked after his water supply and made a weak attempt at keeping books. Farther down the list was the home front with a minimal amount of cooking and housekeeping. Days were never done; neither could he call them his own.

The good will of the Coast Guard had already paved the way for him, so gathering 35 pupils for his first class came easily. Though reaching children remained his pilot project, his patient manner gradually gained the confidence of the entire community. Nevertheless, during long evenings after the storytellers were through elaborating on the exploits of their forefathers, the subject of Stevenson and *tanniks* in general often

Transition

surfaced. With it came a recurring question: Should they be allowed to stay? Changes can be scary. What if their children forgot how to act like proper Eskimos? Someone voiced his misgivings with, "These new people want to upset everything, make everything their way."

"No, I don't think so," another countered. "I heard that the missionary asked to buy skin boots because they were better than the hard kind he wears."

Again the name of Stevenson stilled the storm. Though unable to analyze this missionary to their fullest satisfaction, they nevertheless appreciated his gentle spirit that spoke louder than words.

With home and school taking place in a rear room of the rescue station, the missionary had to man that post too. During his stay in the north he somehow found the time and space to care for literally hundreds of shipwrecked sailors. After four summers of waiting, Stevenson at last saw hope for elbow room when his shipment of building material finally arrived. Almost single-handed and with few tools he turned carpenter and erected a schoolhouse and a mission home before the following winter's storm set in. Special tribute is given here (eternal rewards over there) to Stevenson's wife and children who waited seven years for his return. It was a long wait, especially in view of his having assured them he would be gone no more than 12 months.

Upon graduation from medical school, Dr. Horatio Marsh came with his bride in 1897 to replace Stevenson. History credits Dr. Marsh with saving countless lives, seafarers included. That year winter moved in too soon with early polar ice that crushed eight large whaling vessels. The 300 men who escaped converged on Barrow, filling both the government station and the schoolhouse along with a number of sod dwellings thrown together for the emergency. The Marshes themselves gave up their home and moved in with a native family. There Mrs. Marsh gave birth to their first child. Her husband worked around the clock treating the sick and administering first aid.

Anticipating a tough season due to a shortage of fuel and food, Marsh sent out a frantic plea via the last ship able to plow its way through the ice: "Send medicine and provisions to meet the need of an exploded population...."

It sounded impossible, for how could help possibly arrive in time to save them? His message did, however, get to Washington, D.C. and in quick response the *Bear* was commissioned to sail as far north as possible. How far would that be when winter storms had already set in?

Transition

As expected, the sturdy cutter got icelocked at Nunivak Island, west of Kuskokwim Bay. From there a handful of brave men led by a lieutenant named Jarvis struck out on their own. No way could they corral wild caribou, but they knew of domesticated reindeer that had been imported from Lapland through a joint effort of the Canadian and American governments. The combined herds numbered less than 15 hundred but if these would-be rescuers could round up a third of them, they might beat the threat of starvation farther north.

Cutting overland from Cape Prince of Wales, they met William Lopp, a Congregational missionary who immediately offered his services. Besides being an experienced reindeer herder, his jovial personality would hold them in good stead through the rugged weeks ahead. Heads together over a map, the men charted their course. Barring the worst, they could drive the animals cowboy style overland to Barrow—if they could get them, of course.

Begging and bargaining, they at last netted a final count of 450 reindeer. A fair number came from the government station at Teller, but an Eskimo couple, Charley and Mary Antisarlook, gave their entire herd. The fact that the federal government later reimbursed them with new stock did not, however, minimize their risk of going hungry that year.

At this point Stephen Ivanoff of Unalakleet, a valuable guide who could also double as interpreter should they overtake campers along the route, joined their team. The drive that this assortment of fellows took upon themselves bordered on the unbelievable. Or maybe the ridiculous. Running alongside these half-wild creatures, they managed to keep them together and headed in the right direction. When the animals started to scatter, the men yelled and waved their arms to scare them into a huddle. The dog team hauling their sled of medical supplies and other provisions proved to be a mixed blessing. Skittish of dogs, which reminded them of their number one enemy, wolves, the reindeer panicked whenever the team came in sight. They had a right to be afraid, for several of the stragglers did fall prey to wolf packs. From then on the musher purposely lagged.

The reindeer also stomped the snow in resentment when they were driven contrary to their natural instinct, which seemed always to be facing the wind. They didn't like being continually on the move, either. The herders pushed themselves and the animals equally hard lest a stampede bring about the end of both man and beast. While

Transition

the God-fearing prayed, the others rolled their eyes and wondered what they were headed for. The last round-up maybe? If they ever did make it to the top, maybe it would be only in time to help bury the dead. And with nothing to write home about later, for who would believe their wild tales?

On March 29, 1898, after living under open skies for ten straight weeks, the weary, bedraggled scouts caught sight of Barrow. With only compass and stars to guide them over uncharted wastes, they had hit the target right on. Before he saw them coming, Dr. Marsh had penned one terse entry in his journal: "No food left."

With meat on the hoof and game the men had shot along the way, everyone's needs were more than met. Unfortunately, numerous outsiders didn't sympathize with the rescue operation. Should meat originally intended for the benefit of the native be given to save idle seamen? Dr. Marsh and others involved in the project made no such distinction, but they felt the sting of criticism when even their own churchmen disagreed as to the character of that endeavor. News reporters grabbed the story, some of them going so far as to say that Barrow could have survived quite well without the sacrifice of the poor reindeer. What they didn't realize was that Dr. Marsh took over the supervision of the few animals not needed to meet the emergency and trained local people to care for them. Within a few years the herd increased to over 500 animals. The north slope was never again threatened with wholesale starvation.

Chapter Six

School

Through storm, threat of famine and the diverse upheavals caused by change, school went on. In 1899 the Rev. Samuel Spriggs and his wife came to make Barrow their home for a number of years. In time other teachers joined them, a brave lot to whom the shortage of books was a mere trifle.

Conserving the sparse paper, they called their pupils up to the front to practice writing on a screechy blackboard with stumps of chalk. Mistakes? Use an eraser or, just as well, a parka sleeve. Here again the teachers moved ahead cautiously, for in certain villages farther south the shamans had condemned the use of slates. Don't tell them that they didn't see it happen—marks spirited away right in front of their eyes!

In turn, these educators were educated in the how-to of fitting into already well-established grooves. One of these turnabouts was the polar society's habit of flowing with the 24-hour days of summer and 24-hour nights of winter. Neither did weekends and schooldays make all that much sense to children who had been up twice around the clock. Sleep and get to school when you feel like it. More than once rules had to bend until everyone got a little more used to the idea of a schedule. It took a while before those earlier sessions fell into a semblance of order necessary for group instruction, but classes redeemed themselves by offering a variety of curiosities. The pupils who paid attention had something to go home and tell. When grownups paused in their talk, these young people were quick to interject, "You know what?" "Our teacher said...." "In our books..."

Did the children really want to go to school? Here as everywhere, it is a moot question answered only in the light of whatever else a given day has to offer.

Wise teachers respected the home training that many of the children had already received.

School

Weren't their hunters a resourceful lot even though they didn't know the three R's? A man needed more than pencil and paper to make his way alone through the ice. As for the women, could these newcomers, with their own hands, provide their families with warm, protective clothing? Or design garments so waterproof that a man wedged into his kayak could turn over completely and come up dry? Give the people credit that they had managed over the centuries to keep their race from vanishing off the face of the earth.

Home instruction didn't center entirely around survival. There were proprieties in their culture too, such as the firm rule that no matter how proud one might be, he must never brag. Oldsters told of braggarts who ate their words in the form of sickness or death.

This low profile often misrepresented the native. Besides, words are tools and unless you're skilled in a language it's safest to hold back a bit. Within his own group an Eskimo may get quite vocal with friend and foe alike, but he'd best remember never to boast about himself. Only a few years ago their young people heard of a fleet-footed Inuit who literally chased a caribou until it fell exhausted. The man guarded his story for most of a lifetime. Then some hunters who had witnessed the amazing test of speed and endurance told the man's sons about it.

"We never knew that! Why didn't you tell us, Dad?"

"Because."

"Because why?"

"Because it's wrong to brag. You know that."

Thus it was understandable that people became defensive when the suggestion of a school seemed to imply that they lacked somehow. Semantics might have played its part too. What educators meant when they sent workers, and what the recipients of their efforts heard, weren't always the same.

"Sure, I remember our school," a man from another town and 40 years still angry fumed. "Those teachers weren't fair. They didn't use Eskimo books we could understand, but made us learn to read English books! I didn't like it so I gave them lots of trouble."

This man failed to take two important factors into account. First, his own forefathers hadn't developed a written language. Second, Eskimo languages are based on a far more complicated grammatical structure than English. Teachers would have spent years trying to master it before putting it into written form. So in some villages children who were unhappy with the new language went on a "silence strike." Distraught

School

teachers, homesick and struggling with culture shock, were a little too firm with youngsters who spoke their mother tongue. They enforced "only English or else" that (unless they gave up and took the next boat south) brought them out on top. As a result, many native dialects died out prematurely.

The North Slope fared better when it came to retaining Inupiaq. Either these pupils didn't launch a full-scale cold war, or the teachers handled their problems with foresight. Old English nursery rhymes that often made little sense to the children at least provided a basis for learning to read. After that the pupils practiced small numbers that could be added up to make big numbers. This is the only way, their tutors emphasized, that they could be sure that the fur buyers gave them a fair deal.

Some agreed; others balked. After all, everyone had ten fingers and ten toes. That many digits took care of the number of children one had. It usually sufficed for the seals he got in a day too, for a hunter seldom averaged more than 20—the total of a person. If he were lucky enough to get more, he could mentally borrow (fingers and toes again) from his neighbor.

As for books, their own action-packed stories held a lot more thrills. Reading someone else's writing aloud couldn't hold a flickering candle to

Alone in My Kayak

the art of storytelling. Describing the polar bear coming toward them, the narrator gets down on all fours. Thrusting his head forward, he depicts the long heavy neck peculiar to the lumbering king of the Arctic as he moves slowly toward his audience. Suddenly the speaker springs to his feet with an about-face that identifies him as the hunter. Reaching for his weapon, he leans back for a hefty throw. His actions depict his fear, his instant decision, his exhilaration as single-handedly he saves the lives of everyone in the room. A thrilled audience enters into the distinct pleasure of participating in vivid scenes from actual life.

In the real world, however, no one always comes out the winner. In their search for answers, generations before them had turned to superstitions that smacked of reincarnation. That in turn affected both home and school, for it's not easy to scold a boy who might be grandpa returned. Also, children accustomed to being taught on a one-to-one basis automatically expected further individual attention.

"Look at me. Me!" one after another demanded by word or by gesture as he pointed toward himself.

For all these daily frustrations on both sides, the child who leaped the language barrier enough to form simple sentences earned special privileges.

School

He became the go-between when explanations required more than descriptive hand motions. Men with foresight pushed that child ahead. "Learn all you can," they encouraged. "Times are changing."

The Barrow school no doubt played a big part in Alasurak's move from Wainwright. Training his sons well, he was confident that they could succeed as outdoorsmen like himself. Shuddering involuntarily, the hunter watched a neighbor walking home, dragging his empty sled by a tow line over his shoulder. That man was always poorer than poor. Alasurak had given him dogs, but the lazy one forgot to feed them. And yet, he reflected further, even with folks who really tried, things could go wrong. Like that fellow who coughed all the time before he died. Dirt poor, and he wasn't to blame.

Fate could play some mean tricks. What if one of his sons met with an accident that kept him home? More than following in his footsteps, they must take a leap ahead into an expanding world. The Christian part of the school he'd have to overlook as religion wasn't to be a part of their family discussions anyway. Kignak, however, liked to believe in a God who is good. She had heard said that long ago there was some knowledge of Him, but it had been hushed and His name forgotten. Her talking with Patkotak about those fragments

Alone in My Kayak

from the past planted within the young boy a desire to find out more if he ever had the chance.

Six boys could produce half a dozen reactions to classroom exposure, but the atmosphere, the smell, everything, completely captivated the youngest. With his bent for remembering details, he viewed the books as exciting surprise packages. One day he would have his very own Bible that he could read for himself. Granted, the Good Book stood against scant competition when it came to literary material in their one-room school. Nonetheless, the pupils related more to it than to other tales from faraway lands.

"What shall I read today?" the teacher asked.

No answer.

"Shall I read about David who killed a bear and a giant?"

Pupils lifted their dark eyebrows in assent. Full of action, that story stood out as a favorite. The one about Jesus in an *umiak* too—the time they got hit by a storm. That happened right where they, the children, lived.

When the teacher closed his books and talked about the Lord, Patkotak sat up straighter, hanging on to every word. Conflicting emotions vied for top place when he heard the name of Jesus. No

School

name like that name! Sometimes it made him feel uncomfortable, reminding him of actions he wanted to forget. Like stealing. Lying isn't so bad because everyone does it. Only deep down inside he knew better.

There was something else too. Hearing the name of Jesus made him want to be like Him. When he let that desire in, the uneasy feelings went away. Patkotak concluded that Jesus had to be the best Person ever, for He was the Son of God and at the same time was one with God. The Holy Spirit also worked together with Them, a concept that he found difficult to grasp. Yet They were one and They were good. Not like the evil spirits, the kind that are always wanting to punish poor people with no place to hide.

"The first woman missionary I knew was also my school teacher,"Patkotak recalled. "She often talked to me about Jesus too. One day she asked me, 'Do you have an English name?'

" 'No. My only name is Patkotak,' I answered.

" 'Then I shall give you a good name.'

" 'A good name? What is it?'

" 'You shall be called Paul, after the apostle Paul.'

"As soon as she said it, my heart began to beat fast and hard. I understood that Paul was a good man. He served the Lord with all his heart, with all the strength he had. Could I be like him? Could I get to know God and serve Him too?"

Maybe by giving him that name his teacher had implied that possibility. Or was it only that the two names blended well? He would like to know, but how could one be so bold as to ask? Paul Patkotak hesitated....

No, he'd only fumble for words. Besides, it was best to play it safe a while. What if the *angakok* resented his meddling in the white man's religion and turned everyone against him? There! Fear raised its ugly head again. The teenager who wanted to be brave cringed as he imagined the worst. He wished he had that something the believers called "faith." Or maybe it was "grace." Whatever....

"Give me time," he said to himself. "I'll find out more about Jesus when I grow up."

Secretly the teenager dreamed about going "Outside" (also called the "South 48") for book learning. As the longing grew and began to take shape, there came with it a conviction that in some miraculous way it would evolve into reality.

The name of Jesus gave him that too—a hope. It wasn't like when he went hunting and hoped to get a seal. This was a deeper hope that warmed the heart.

Chapter Seven

Marooned

The teenager lifted his paddle noiselessly from the water, swinging it over to the other side of his kayak. He set a small ice cake twirling which in turn struck a larger one. The gentle rocking motions never disturbed a walrus sunning itself on a huge ice floe. The young hunter had purposely slipped by, pleased with himself for not waking the animal. Not that it mattered, for a walrus wouldn't attack unless its life was threatened—but a successful hunter practices silence.

Patkotak's parents had moved back to Wainwright for the season, temporarily halting his schooling. If he felt disappointed, he never said so. Besides, with his zest for hunting he could stay out for hours on end. Then came this special day when he could hardly wait to get home to show off his prize. He envisioned the surprised look on his parents' faces when he came with his first seal in tow. Although trying to appear nonchalant, pride oozed from all of his pores. This first profitable hunt by himself amounted to his taking that initial step into the adult world, proving that, given a few years, he would be able to provide for a family of his own.

Sixth son smiled. This was living! The ways of the veteran hunters had always challenged him. This perpetual eagerness to learn something new combined with an ability to see tasks close at hand placed him in line for advancement. Only he dared not ask, for such privileges belong only to those who earn the right to participate. The coveted invitation, that would make him one of the youngest fellows ever to be included in a full-scale whale hunt lay just around the corner.

When the late January sun peeked over the southern horizon, the cold strengthened. No matter, for as daylight hours increased everyone found more reason to spend time out of doors. By the last of February the men were into serious talk

Marooned

about whaling, and preparation for it had to begin weeks before the hunt itself became reality. Boat owners dug their *umiaks* out of snowdrifts to examine them against last season's damages. Even when lying idle, the boats took a beating from the winter storms that often left them in worse shape than when in daily use. Nosy polar bears also did their share of damage to boats left unattended. Holes or tears must be mended, broken paddles replaced. Hunters spent hours cleaning and oiling their whaling guns. Harpoons designed to be driven into a whale by human strength also had to be sharpened. A tough air balloon, fashioned from the stomach of a seal and attached to the harpoon by a long tow line, had to be flawless. These blown-up gut balls dragging against an injured animal's reserve strength cut down its get-away speed. So refurbish the old; and if necessary, make new.

Skilled fingers felt for weak spots in the rawhide lacing of their sleds that must be reinforced to bear the more than average weight. The best of their weathermen checked the ice daily, studied the skies, compared temperatures. As soon as they figured that the ocean ice was about to break up, the whalers quickly loaded their skin boats and camping gear onto sleds. A single team can pull several hundred pounds, but shore ice buckling under pressure often formed a chain of

Alone in My Kayak

ridges that presented a formidable barrier. Then team joined with team, pulling together as one to get over the top.

Mush! Dogs pulled and men pushed, everyone straining to transport one huge load after another over the ridges to smoother ice near a strip of open water—a break in the ice known as "the open lead." They set up camp on the "fast ice" that still clung to the shore. On the other side of this narrow waterway lay the pack ice that wind and current would move out later. The yearly migration of whales followed this natural open water channel, surfacing to breathe or blow.

The distance to camp varied from one whaling season to the next, with a site sometimes in view of the village or as far as 15 miles away. Often entire families—wives, children and grandparents—accompanied the hunters. They pitched their tents, cooking over open fires while waiting to witness this annual contest between man and the untamed Arctic.

For those directly involved, *umiaks* propped on their sides served as windbreaks close to the water's edge. The younger fellows applied their extra energy whirling bolas at flocks of geese and eider ducks flying overhead, bringing down enough for their fresh meat supply. Others took turns sitting at a post that afforded a clear view to the south and west, squinting their eyes to slits to avoid glaring light reflections off the ice. Sooner or later a smooth rounded back was certain to surface in the open water.

When the scouts' cry, "*agvig!*" (whale) rang through the camp, the men who were to paddle leaped into their *umiaks* and moved out within seconds. Considerably larger than kayaks, these boats nevertheless moved quickly, skimmed along almost without sound in pursuit of the giant mammal. Each person in the foremost *umiak*, the one making the strike, understood his position. This was no free-for-all. As they neared their prey, one man stood ready with harpoon or gun. The crew worked in perfect timing, the rowers in rhythm, alert to obey their captain's orders implicitly. Lives depended on faultless cooperation. The one who failed on this point faced dismissal for the duration of the season, a public disgrace.

If the key man didn't hit the whale right on, it foamed up some real action. The angry creature might treat its assailants to a long and unplanned ride before finally giving up. Or it might deal a backhanded slap of its monstrous tail. Rarely, however, did anyone get whipped by a fluke that on a 30-ton whale could measure 20 feet across. These hunters were professionals in their field.

Alone in My Kayak

So what if the hunt invited danger? The need for food as well as the challenge made the weakest among them stand strong. With the contest finally over and in their favor, *umiaks* convoyed to pull the animal close to shore. After that the grand tug of war began. Dragging a great mammal measuring 30 to 50 feet in length required the combined might of men, women and dogs. "All hands! Heave-ho!"

Moving it even a fraction of an inch was worth a cheer! Too often a great mammal's tonnage crushed the shore ice just as the people thought they had it beached. Before the days of block and tackle, men sometimes worked from their boats, hacking away chunks of blubber to lighten the load. Even today hauling thousands of pounds to a solid base for cutting can take 10 to 12 hours or longer. The giant must be taken care of immediately. Though early spring has enough winter in it to resemble a great deep-freeze, time loss can mean spoilage. Warm gases building up within that huge body could produce what is called a "stink whale," a tragic waste.

Hoping for the best, bystanders hang around. At last the captain responsible for the successful strike leaps on the whale's fluke and dashes up its back like a winner in the game of "king of the mountain." In that crowning moment he's applauded as victor until a broad sweep of his arms tells those below that their moment also has come.

Everyone handy with a knife rushes forward, slashing through the tough skin, paring off a chunk of tasty *muktuk* for himself. Afterwards he trims off mouth-size pieces for eager youngsters ducking their way between the adults. The mild flavor of this "chewing gum" has often been compared to that of walnuts. It also rates high as a delicacy and in nutritional value. Thick and rubbery, it exercises the chewing muscles while acting as an effective tooth cleaner. *Muktuk* receives credit for toothaches being almost unknown among their children—during the pre-sugar era, of course.

The proper handling of thousands of pounds of meat kept crews working for days. After carefully removing that first precious layer, they scored off the thick blubber and threw it to one side to be used for fuel. It made a hot fire as grease spit into the flames, and without the unpleasant smell one might expect. After that they cut into the fine-grained red meat that would provide them with literally thousands of meals. Some of the stronger men stayed with the job for 24 hours before dropping, parka and boots still on, for a nap. Spirits zoomed to a new high with men laughing as they recounted every move of their recent conquest. One incident reminded them of another, of last year's record-breaker or of one that got away. Story led to legend; a lighthearted remark became a long-standing joke. Someone climbing on top of the whale to show off slipped and fell. Hey there, enough clowning—get on with the work!

Again the party moves into full swing. The whaling captain and crew that struck first (which sometimes has to be proven by a marked charge or harpoon found in the animal) got choice portions of meat. Generous amounts were likewise allotted to participating crews as well as to older people no longer contributing to the hunt as they once did. Though poorer families might have done without at other times, never during this springtime spree. Children darted here and there, sliding down the whale's back or crawling into its mouth for their own version of hide-and-seek. They ran beside the sleds loaded with meat being transported to the village, a task more difficult than the initial setting up of the camps. Backing off as the men struggled to get their loads over ice barriers, the boys and girls in festive mood turned to tease the next sledder. They hadn't had so much fun since last whaling season!

All the while the work went on, for nothing was to be wasted. From the stomach of the whale they garnered clams, shrimp and other delicacies that hadn't yet been digested. Women with their pie-shaped knives cut chunks of meat to fit into their cook pots. Thus began *nulakatuq* (whale days) with its feasting and competitive games that lasted about a week.

The conclusion of these holidays ushered in the change of seasons with its pleasant variety of activities. Although older folk seldom complained about the cold, the continual fight to stay alive wore on their reserves. Generally speaking, the hunters fared better than those confined to the village. For women cooped up too long in sod igloos, this long-awaited break saved their sanity.

In Patkotak's day, the short summer called for camping away from the confines of winter living. Housewives added to their store of take-home food by gathering bird eggs, and by netting or hooking Arctic char (a small-scaled trout) and candlefish. They ate their smaller catches fresh or laid them out to dry with the aid of wind and sun. At low tide, especially after a storm, women and children combed the beaches looking for tidefoods and other goodies from the sea tossed up by the waves. Sleepy-eyed dogs basking in the sun required less food; pups ran loose to fend for themselves. How easy then to forgive that past winter for its insensitive hardships.

The spring following his fourteenth birthday, Patkotak's family moved back to their home in Wainwright for the summer months. As his older brothers established their own homes, he gradually picked up their responsibilities by providing at least part of the family's daily fare.

Then came the big moment. At the beginning of autumn his uncle Takpak, an outstanding hunter, invited the teenager to join his crew. Though fewer whales are taken when they're heading south, he would try to get extra meat for winter. Not expecting a hard freeze for some weeks to come, several boats carrying no more provision than absolutely necessary started out together. After arriving at their destination some distance southwest of the village, the hunters chose a huge ice floe for their campsite. Now all they had to do was settle down and wait.

Somehow the boat captains had miscalculated, or the migrating whales outsmarted them. Whatever the reason, rations began to run low before the hunters caught sight of a blow. At last they agreed that one of the *umiaks* must return to the village the next day. Unless the men ran into an unexpected delay, they could get back again before nightfall with food enough for the crews to continue their watch.

While some of the men griped about their bad luck, others shrugged it off. Regardless of first reactions, it was at best a boring inconvenience.

Marooned

They'd much rather get on with the game. But worry? What for? Nothing in wind or sky suggested a change in weather. Nor was this the first time that whales had exercised their prerogative to come when they pleased. With that matter settled, the hunters crawled into their warm caribou sled bags under *umiak* shelters. Oblivious to the slightest hint of impending danger, they stretched out for the night.

Morning light revealed a startling situation. A drastic drop in temperature had frozen the "open leads," turning the channels into solid ice. Plans cancelled! To either walk or try to drag their boats over 75 miles of ice to Wainwright was unthinkable for men with near-empty stomachs. Although aware of their serious predicament, these past masters of the game doggedly refused to get upset about it. *Keep your courage up, fellows. You've been in tight spots before. The weather will change.*

"But that didn't happen," Patkotak recalled. "It never warmed up and no strong wind came to help open things up.

"My uncle Takpak who was captain of our boat had much experience as a hunter and he became uneasy. The whole day went by with no change, only ice getting thicker. The cold meant danger when we were so low on food.

Alone in My Kayak

"In the evening my uncle came to me and said, 'We have only one hope left. We must pray to God in Heaven for help. I have heard that He can answer prayer and do what no one else can do. You go out on the ice and ask Him for a miracle to save us. Do it now so we can get home safely.'

"My uncle was not a Christian, but he had gone to meetings at the Presbyterian mission in our village. There he had heard that God answers prayer when we have need. But because he was afraid people would make fun of him, he ordered me to go out and pray.

" 'Go out and lay down on the ice,' he said. 'Ask God to open the ice and make a way for us to get through.'

"My uncle meant what he said. I understood the big trouble we were in. I got up from our shelter under the boat and went out and lay down on the ice. I had never prayed that kind of a prayer before and I wasn't sure how I was supposed to do it. But I did as my uncle said, asking God to make a way for us.

"It was getting late. After I prayed I went straight back to the boat and crawled under the skin I used for a blanket. It never looked like anything was going to happen. Most of the men didn't know about my little talk with God. One after another they fell asleep. No need to keep watch when we were locked in by ice.

"A couple of hours after midnight we heard a sharp cracking sound far away. It sounded like ice breaking up. Right away hunters woke up and jumped to their feet.

"Someone shouted, 'Look! A break in the ice! It's getting bigger and it's coming this way!'

"All the men strained to see out into the night. They could hardly believe their own eyes. The ice was parting! The break began at the shore—something very unusual—and opened exactly in the direction of our camp. As the lead opened past us, we saw that it was just wide enough for us to put our boats into the water. The lead kept on breaking open in the northeast direction from which we had come. All other ice stayed frozen and never moved.

"We hurried to put the *umiaks* in water—nine boats in one long row—and began our homeward journey. It took three days. We rowed in shifts so we could have turns to rest. A steady wind was blowing and the temperature stayed the same. Our one lead, it remained open all the way and exactly wide enough for our skin boats.

"When we reached land near our home, it was at the very spot we started from. We got home about midnight. We see a lantern in the distance, then two lanterns. Young men were out.

"We called, 'Tell the village we have come home. Tell them all of us are safe.'

"How could that happen? None of the old hunters had ever seen anything like it. They knew that it is against nature for such a lead to open and stay open in that kind of freezing weather. Everyone understood that a higher power had worked for us, but what that higher power was no one tried to say.

"For me it was an open sign of God's power. He had answered my prayer and performed a miracle to save us. That was the first of many miracles I was to see in answer to prayer. My God is real!"

Chapter Eight

Outside

Kignak's pride must have been mixed with humble appreciation as she watched her children mature. She looked at her youngest who, in spite of his beggared start in life, had grown into a healthy teenager on his way to becoming a successful hunter.

Having already worked for his uncle Takpak, Patkotak stood in line for the coveted invitation to join another crew after his family moved back to Barrow. The whaling captain who sought him out, however, had more than an extra pair of strong arms in mind when he took on this helper. Growing up before schools came to the north, he intended to make up, at least in part, for that lack while waiting long hours out on the ice. He couldn't read, but he could listen. "Patkotak, open the Book. Tell us what it says," the devout captain ordered as he handed the newest crew member a copy of God's Word.

Patkotak didn't have to be asked twice! The youth read for all to hear, stories about Jesus, teachings of a universal gospel relevant to every culture. Nothing would he rather do than pore over those pages, turning them with respect. In his time alone he went back over unfamiliar words and phrases, hoping by context to dig out hidden meanings. Like a friend, a book takes time to get to know.

"You believe that last story you read, Patkotak?"

"Believe it? Yes. The Bible is true." "But some of those things couldn't happen," the older man countered. "They don't happen today. You know that."

"Anyway, I still think they could happen. I can't explain it, but I still believe them."

His leader nodded and smiled. He had only been teasing, maybe testing, the young hunter. He too believed.

Outside

After reading the Bible for an hour—real effort for one with a limited command of English—Patkotak closed it carefully so the playful wind wouldn't ruffle its smooth pages. Pausing to rest, his solemn brown eyes seemed to look beyond the horizon. Leaning back, he breathed deeply. This was living! Come to think of it, that's what he said to himself when he came in from a successful hunt too. Obviously he wanted the best of both worlds.

Had he chosen to make himself that vulnerable, he would have also admitted to an elusive, hard-to-pinpoint loneliness. Never was he completely free or one hundred percent happy—as if something far away beckoned him. Whenever he met a missionary or held a Bible, that call grew stronger. Try as he would, there was no shaking off an indefinable emotion that made him both glad and sad.

"Because I couldn't go to school all the time," Patkotak explained, "I didn't read well. After I finished the seventh grade, I wished I could go to school somewhere else. I wanted to get more education so I could understand the big words in the Bible. I talked to Mrs. Spriggs who was my teacher at the time and told her that I wanted to go to school, but I got no money."

Aware that ambitions too easily realized may be less appreciated, the teacher didn't offer to help him financially. The depth of his desire had to be proven not only to her, but to himself as well. He himself must take the first step toward the unfolding of his dreams. She also foresaw what could trigger an avalanche of adventurous young people wanting a free trip south. After he had earned his fare, she would contact friends in Seattle who could help him find a place to live.

While he hesitated, Mrs. Spriggs interjected a thought. "You have foxes here—white fox, cross fox, silver fox and red fox. Foxes are worth money. Why don't you trap foxes and sell the skins?"

Why didn't he? The student nodded, giving his teacher a wide smile as plans began formulating in his head.

"I know I have to do something," he later explained, "so I spoke to my dad. 'I wish I could go trapping sometime. I want to get foxes.'

"My older brother showed me how to make a trap in the ground. We used a piece of wood with a heavy rock balanced on it. We covered it with a thin layer of snow so the fox wouldn't see it. He breaks through when he walks over it. He falls and the rock hits him on the head and kills him. That is Eskimo kind of trap. My brother gave me steel traps too.

"I asked my dad to make me big long snowshoes about three or four feet long so I can use

Outside

them to walk over soft snow. When my dad finished the snowshoes, I said, 'Now I am ready to go.'

"I woke up early Saturday morning as there was no school on Saturday. I put my traps, maybe dozens of them, in a bag. I packed the bag along with a big rifle on my back. I put on my new snowshoes and walked about ten miles over the tundra, flat country, to where the foxes were. I was about 17 years old that time. I saw fox tracks where they had walked around a knoll. There I made Eskimo traps and set steel traps too.

"I went over my trap line every Saturday and when I saw a fox in a trap it would make me happy. I said to myself, 'When I catch enough to buy my fare to go Outside, I will be glad.'

"Over many Saturdays I checked my traps and sometimes I was lucky. But sometimes that big thief, the wolverine, got there first—broke the trap and took the fox."

The wolverine, smaller than a wolf, is feared and hated more than any other animal of the north. Indian folklore declared that vicious one with its consuming desire to destroy to be the devil incarnate. After killing an animal several times its size, it doesn't satisfy its own hunger first. Instead, as if to prove its mastery, this rogue of nearly limitless endurance drags its prey some distance before finally savoring the spoils of victory.

Alone in My Kayak

Rarely known to attack people, the wolverine nonetheless takes apparent delight in harassing them. One account told for fact involves an Alaskan trapper who lived in what he considered a bear-proof cabin. When he returned to his one-room home, he saw that he had been host to an unbidden guest. Tracks told him that a wolverine had broken in. Obviously most interested in food supplies, it had ransacked the place. Satisfying its hunger, however, didn't pacify its ugly nature. The rascal literally vandalized the place, tearing open boxes and scattering foodstuffs in every direction.

As was his habit, the trapper had left his snowshoes outdoors before going in. After boarding up the windows, he went to bed tired and discouraged. When he got up the following morning, he ate his breakfast, then went out to put on his snowshoes. The rawhide lacing had been torn to shreds! Fresh tracks once more identified the culprit.

Knowing he shouldn't be traveling any distance without proper footwear, the bewildered trapper hesitated. Nevertheless, after securely bolting the door he hurried on his way. He must at least check his line before his scheming enemy beat him to it.

The completion of his rounds verified his worst hunches. The cunning wolverine had indeed gone

Outside

ahead to destroy every trap he had set. Defeated and almost beside himself with pent-up rage, the poor fellow trudged the long route through deep snow back to his cabin. Not soon enough. His earlier visitor beat him to it and somehow managed to tear its way in again, creating even more havoc than before.

In spite of such stories and his own experiences with that wicked one, Patkotak continued trapping. His mother used the damaged pelts for parka trim. Marketable ones he kept for himself. First he turned the pelt inside out like a glove, drawing it over a smooth flat board so he could scrap off fatty tissue clinging to the parchment-like skin. When it was thoroughly dried, he took it off the board and turned it right side again. Holding it at arm's length he shook it hard making the long guard hairs stand up. A few of these would buy his ticket to Seattle.

"When I had 19 nice white fox skins, I said to my dad, 'Can I go Outside, so I can go to school?'"

"He said, 'Yes, you can go. Your older brother will take care of us.'"

Patkotak had jumped the first hurdle. Next he must find a way south. No passenger ships ever sailed as far north as Barrow. The only boat he was sure about was the Coast Guard cutter. Day after day the young man scanned the horizon for the *Bear*, affectionately labeled "the mercy ship." Local folks, picking up on another of her traits, dubbed her "big smoke ship." The federal government, when it purchased the vessel of 1874 vintage, was thinking of practicality rather than beauty. Although sailing partly under canvas, the two-cylinder engine also required 392 tons of coal for its Seattle-Barrow round trip. When fuel bins spilled over, the fireman ordered the rest stacked on deck. In spite of her sooty appearance, however, the old cutter had won lots of hearts. Faithful, never complaining, it earned more fame in the Arctic than anything else afloat. Seattle's journalist, R.H. Calkins, penned her praise: "To the native she meant law, order, civilization, and justice."

Patkotak stepped confidently up to the captain. He wanted to go Outside, he stated, to further his education. Listening with his heart, the older man studied the younger's face. Clearly etched was a sincerity he couldn't refuse. Even though the ship wasn't meant to double as a passenger carrier, the captain could make room for one more. If this eager chap someday returned to help his own people, they would have carried out another worthy mission.

"All right, young man, you have my permission. You be ready and you can come with us."

Outside

An excited Patkotak rode in a small boat out to the ship at anchor. Climbing up the rope "Jacob's ladder" that hung against its side, he swung himself on board with his few personal belongings in two bags. One held his clothes, the other his precious fox skins. Deep in his pocket he kept a slip of paper with an address the teacher had given him. Destination: Seattle.

"So I got ready to go on a government boat that would take me south as far as Nome for nothing. Never cost me a cent," he added with penny-saved-penny-earned satisfaction.

The fireman had already stoked the burner. Its two huge cylinders went into noisy action as the *Bear* headed toward open sea. Paul Patkotak tingled to the throbbing sensation of pistons hammering away until the whole ship vibrated. Those iron elbows never got tired. To think that men could invent machinery more powerful than 20 oarsmen in perfect rhythm! While the crew busied themselves with their assigned duties, the voyager lingering near the railing waved until he could no longer distinguish family or friends.

Sailing west and south, the vessel ran into heavier seas. Seeing that another deck hand wasn't necessary, Patkotak wisely stayed out of the way. He spent hours gazing over the open water,

Alone in My Kayak

facing the wind and thrilling to the spray that splashed over the bow. Tiring of that, he made his way to the stern to relax, or ventured to the pilot house where he could watch the skipper. These fellows knew so much!

Later they passed his old home village of Wainwright and other spots he would have liked to visit, but the ship made no stops unless absolutely necessary. The fall equinoctial storms would be moving in shortly. Passing through Kotzebue Sound they rounded Seward Peninsula and entered Norton Sound. When activity on board suddenly picked up, one of the crew pointed out the gold rush town of Nome that lay just ahead.

Before they dropped anchor, a concerned captain again counseled his young passenger. "This is the place I told you about, Paul. We have to stop at several small villages before we wind up our summer's work, so you must get off here at Nome. If you are careful, you'll be all right. Do you remember what else I told you?"

"Yes. I wait for Alaska Steamship Company's big ship. They will take me to Seattle."

"But you will have to ask them. Right?"

"I understand. I wait for the ship. As soon as I can, I will talk to them."

Outside

The captain gave Patkotak a kindly smile. It seemed almost unfair to leave him there by himself, but they had other assignments. After they anchored, the lone passenger made the rounds of the crew to say good-bye to brief but pleasant friendships. If seamen who slapped him on the back slipped in a salty expression while encouraging him to "hang in there," no harm done. He wouldn't have understood anyway. What they didn't say aloud, they hoped in their hearts—that he wouldn't have to learn too much too fast.

From Patkotak's side, he would miss the fatherly captain and congenial crew. What he didn't know was that before the day was done he'd also wish for his own bunk and meals prepared by a real cook. Standing alone between his two long stretches of travel gave him a queasy turning in the pit of his stomach. Boyish dreams began crumbling. He had taken one awful plunge! What if ice moved in too soon and the company ship never showed up? If he did get all the way to Seattle like he planned, would the Outside be too different from what he expected? Although the term "culture shock" might not have been coined yet, it socked him hard, right in the middle.

On shore at Nome Patkotak guarded his cumbersome wallet of furs carefully. Its peculiar yet not altogether unpleasant odor would have told

Alone in My Kayak

any native or fur buyer what it contained. To his advantage, most of the drifters in Nome were interested in gold, not pelts. He looked around hesitantly, wondering where he could stay. Unfortunately, the teacher who arranged for his arrival at a stateside seaport had overlooked the possibility of a drawn-out layover enroute. Had they thought of it, a letter of introduction would have put the traveler under the protective wing of Congregationalists, Methodists or Episcopalians active there at the time.

Patkotak stood dumfounded as with one sweeping glance he took in more people than he had seen in a lifetime. An estimated population of 20,000 were crammed into a ramshakle town that had begun to age before recovering from growing pains, its worn boardwalks creaking with misery. Most of the *cheechakos* (newcomers) had arrived trembling with gold fever after news of a big strike leaked out. First reports told of a Swede named Johanson, who discovered the yellow stuff in 1894. Greed fed on greed as entrepreneurs hurriedly salvaged old vessels from "bone yards." Anything that would float got pressed into service, freighting men and cargo north.

With the gold rush reaching its peak by 1910, the boom city began to feel the pinch of decline. When Patkotak arrived about a year later the scene

Outside

could still be described as continuing chaos. Afraid someone might stake their claims if they left, prospectors brushed aside any possibility of taking so much as a brief vacation. With housing scarce, they huddled together in tent cities that lined the river banks, spilling their refuse onto the beach— waiting for a chance to "make it big." A lot of men came north totally unprepared to face physical hardships. Adding to the uncertainties of a society without any social services, a number of gold seekers went beserk with loneliness. The old Alaskan expression of someone having "missed too many boats" came from their seeing the worst happen all too often. It likewise went ill for others who, though keeping their sanity, fell to various get-rich-quick schemes. Nor is there much to say for those who stooped to devising ways of their own for trapping the less wary. The number who "made it" was comparatively small.

The young visitor from the far north hadn't grown up in a particularly sheltered environment. But this? He stared in shocked amazement at the moral decay and utter confusion around him. A collage of vices clamored for his participation: drinking, fighting, brawls, scantily-clothed dancers on stage.... He couldn't stomach more.

His view of his own race likewise broadened as he got acquainted with those of the Inupiaq language

Alone in My Kayak

group whose strange dialects he barely understood. When Yupik Eskimos greeted him, they might just as well have talked Chinese. The word *Eskimo* encompassed a lot more than he had ever realized. Never could he master so many tongues of native Alaska! He'd have to work harder than ever to perfect his English. Nevertheless, friendly natives gave him a corner where he could rest when weary of walking the streets. The women curiously inspected his boots and the cut of his parka; styles and designs unique to each locale gave handmade items special significance.

Biding his time in Nome convinced Paul Patkotak that the mad lust for gold hadn't improved the natives' lot either. Its inroads had already altered their life style more than going to school ever did.

Patkotak summed up his experiences: "Life among the whites there made me wonder if I really ought to travel on. If Americans in Seattle were like these fellows, then I wouldn't be happy living there. Again I remembered the missionaries in our village up north. I was sure that in Seattle I'd find more good people like the Christians I had come to know back home. So I comforted myself with the hope that in the end all would go well.

"It seems like we get used to things," he added with insight. "That's not always the best either.

Outside

While I walked around those two weeks waiting for a ship, I was a little bit tempted. What if I tried my luck at gold panning too? Maybe I could get enough ahead to get me off to a really good start. Before long I realized that I didn't stand much chance with those guys. They were smart and they wouldn't care what happened to me. They think only of themselves.

"The same time a little voice inside me warned me to stay away from people who live like that. God was watching over me, for He knew that down deep in my heart I wanted to do what was right.

"At last here comes Alaska Steamship Company boat. I could hardly wait for it to tie up. I went over and talked to one of the officers.

" 'I want to go Outside, down to Seattle by boat,' I said.

" 'You got money?' he asked. 'You can go if you got money to pay your fare. Thirty-five dollars second class.'

" 'I have no money, but I have fox skins.'

"He said, 'Yes, you can go. We like fox skins. They are worth money.'

"When I showed him my skins, I asked how many he wanted.

"He said, 'Five.'

"I gave him the skins and he was glad. I was glad too. I was on my way to Seattle. I still had 14 skins to sell so I would have money to live on."

The company boat which had brought men north in search of gold was taking a teenager south in search of God.

Chapter Nine

Saved

How could this venturer from the far north describe his first impressions of Seattle, a city hailed by gold seekers as "the gateway to Alaska"? Its wide paved streets made the tundra trails he knew look like a joke. Neither did its houses and apartment buildings resemble the subterranean dwellings of his childhood. Moving into an urban society turned out to be one tough assignment.

Paul Patkotak earned his room and board in a private home by doing chores. During his free hours he often walked back down to the harbor to take in the sights, sounds and smells of Puget

Alone in My Kayak

Sound. Strolling out on a pier, he stared in unabashed admiration at sturdy halibut schooners unloading fish or taking ice into their holds. Farther over, full-sailed ships tugged at their ropes as if begging to be set free. But these larger vessels never dwarfed his honest pride in the simpler handmade kayaks and *umiaks* that had served his people well for generations.

Edging his way toward a whaler, the shy newcomer made friends with sailors who had plied the waters of coastal Alaska. "Come here, lad," a burly fellow beckoned. "We've got *muktuk*. Take as much as you want."

Sailors spending months away from home understood the association one makes with a familiar diet. More than pleasing to the taste buds, it satisfies an almost emotional craving for food to which a person is accustomed.

"*Quyanaq!*" lay on his tongue, but he caught himself in time to switch to a carefully clipped, "Thank you!"

The familiar figure on his usual route met a kind word here and there, or an offer of fresh fruit or baked goodies, all which brightened his days. Yet no one seemed to penetrate his shell of reserve. Lonely chap, what was he looking for?

Doggedly pursuing an education turned out to be a bugaboo. As a matter of fact, had he known.... All right, what he had done, he had done. Paul Patkotak sat in on classes at Seattle Free Methodist Seminary (now Seattle Pacific University) for two winters. The stranger among them who couldn't register as a full-fledged student was left to sit quietly at the back of a classroom. He took in little of what was said, for everyone talked too fast. He barely grasped the first half of a sentence before the speedsters raced on to the next. Worse yet, he had to stand on the sidelines watching others play. If only they would include him! No background for picking up the rules to their games left the impression that perhaps he wasn't all that smart.

"In school I had many problems," Patkotak reflected with a twinge of sadness. "The language gave me headaches, real headaches, and the other pupils made fun of my speech. My clothes were different too, but I made up my mind to hold out. I had come south to learn about the Bible. Whenever I heard someone read it, my hunger grew. More than anything else in the world, I wanted to experience what the Bible talked about."

It looked as if Patkotak's journey to find God was a fiasco. What he didn't realize was that the seeker was being sought. He and God would find each other.

"After I had been in school two years," Patkotak continued, "I began to think, 'I can't stand this much longer!' I wanted to meet God. I had read so much about Him. I had gone to meetings in different churches, but the need of my heart was not met. I had learned much, but I didn't really know God.

"One day as I stood on the street I saw many churches. I looked around again. There was another church and another and another—almost without moving my feet. There was a street meeting going on too.

"An old man came up to me and said, 'Where are you from? What are you looking for?'

"I said, 'I am from Alaska. I came down here to get an education. I thought I would go to school here so I would be able to read the big words in the Bible.'

" 'Are you hungry for God?' he asked me.

"I said, 'Yes,' and he said, 'I'll show you where to go.'

"That sounded good to me. I needed help at that time. I was thinking because I had read in Revelation that the Lord doesn't want a lukewarm people. He wants them hot.

Saved

"I said to myself, 'I want to be among those who are hot.' I didn't want to be spitten out.

"We came to the Apostolic Faith mission—that was in the year 1913. When I stepped inside, I felt something as though someone said to me, 'These are the people you are looking for.' That came to me so plainly.

"I glanced around and saw a long bench under the pulpit. Nobody sat on it. I wondered what that long bench was for. Every person who came in went to his seat and dropped to his knees. I watched them closely. I said to myself, 'There is something to that.'

"When there were a lot of people in church, the preacher came to the pulpit and started the service. What beautiful singing! It was like the whole congregation was lifted up in righteousness and peace. I alone sat back in my darkness.

"Suddenly I saw why I couldn't take part in their worship even though I knew some of the songs from before. My childhood in the Arctic rose before me like high walls. These walls were what hindered me from the heavenly view that those around me had. Small thievery, lying, disobedience, and believing in witch doctors had built up to close me in.

Alone in My Kayak

"Although I knew that these things weren't good, I hadn't realized before what they really meant. Now they rose up like the mountains south of Wainwright. Then it seemed like I heard the evil spirits screaming their threats of trouble and death if I dared forsake my trust in them. At once I understood that those spirits were dangerous. They had hindered me from seeing God's plan for my life and were also blinding my people in the north—keeping them from understanding God's plan of salvation, keeping them from learning to know Him as the missionaries did.

"As if that wasn't enough, dark clouds from my trying to attend classes settled down over those mountains until I could see nothing else. What was it? When some of the other students had noticed my strange dress and manners, they had begun calling me 'Eskimo dog' and other belittling names. The boys often made fun of me, hitting me and kicking me.

"The holy atmosphere in which I found myself revealed the truth. When I thought of my school comrades, my heart became filled with anger and hate. I felt that I had every right to hate them. God put His finger on that hate. He let me know that it was one of the sins that kept me away from Him.

"God didn't stop with that. He showed me another Man who suffered shame and reproach. He was spit on and beaten and then crucified, but

He never opened His mouth. Suddenly a little light peeked through the dark clouds that threatened me. From that light stepped Jesus and His presence made the dark cloud disappear. He set His scarred feet on the mountains and they melted like wax.

"I found myself in an open place in front of Jesus. Love and peace streamed from Him to me. Then I understood that Jesus was bruised to set me free and carry away the judgment that I should have carried. The spirit world that I had feared lost its power because of His nearness. I had at last met the One who has power over evil!

"Then came testimony time and a lot of people got up, sometimes five at once. One kept right on talking until the rest sat down. A colored sister testified and said she thanked God for saving her soul. She said that God doesn't look on the color of our skin. Something in my heart began to move—to start up. The sin I had committed against the Word of God began to move in my heart. I was surely under conviction. I felt like I was shaking.

"The preacher started preaching, but I didn't hear much of what he said. I was hungry for him to stop preaching so I could pray. I wanted to call on God to have mercy on me a sinner, to take sin out of my heart.

Alone in My Kayak

"At the altar call I went forward, to the long bench in front of the pulpit. I was crying, asking the Lord to forgive me of my sins. I prayed for about five minutes, asking God to take the sin out of my heart. He heard that prayer and I knew the sins were all gone. I felt light, just like a balloon, no weight on me. My sins were all gone, washed away by the blood of Jesus.

"After that I stood up and I walked right up to the platform. I pulled on the preacher's sleeve. I said, 'I want to say something.'

"I faced the people in the congregation which I had never seen before in my life. I told them that I had found Jesus. I knew it! I felt good that night. I felt like I wanted to keep talking about Jesus. When I was talking I heard somebody say, 'Praise God!' I felt like talking more.

"Someone in the church said, 'Glory to Jesus!' It made me feel lighter, so I talked some more. When the meeting was over they came around me and shook hands with me. I told them, 'I am a full-blooded Eskimo, hungry for the Lord, and now I have found Him.'

"I remembered the words of Jesus that He said to Thomas, 'Blessed are they that have not seen, and yet have believed.' From that day on to this I am happy and I have always witnessed for Him. I read His Word every day because He is so good and He is so real to me.

"The Lord often talked to me," Patkotak continued. "I didn't have many others to share with, so it gave me lots of time with my heavenly Father. That way I learned to know His voice and to do what He said. Always He speaks quietly, but plainly. Other voices come with unrest, so it isn't hard to tell them apart.

"Just as the Lord called Abraham to leave his people and his father's house, so the Lord called me back home to witness for Him. 'Tell them what you have found in Me,' He said. 'The Word you give will not return empty. If you believe My Word, it will be fulfilled just as I promised.' "

The realization of that call back to his own people wouldn't come right away, for first he needed a boost to his shattered morale. A couple of years in a government boarding school for native Americans filled in some of his educational gaps and helped him to realize his worth as an individual—both native and American with no apologies for either.

Later Patkotak moved to Portland, Oregon, to work and attend Bible classes at the downtown mission. Sheltered among fellow believers who called him "Brother Paul," he became something of a mascot. His personality blossomed under the protective wing of a body that placed emphasis on lifting the down-and-outer. Drifter, shoe clerk, housewife and corporate executive were grouped alike under one heading—sinners saved by grace. The rich man cared less about his gold watch chain, while the tramp who had ridden rails got cleaned up and looked for a job. In the middle of this conglomerate of friends, the young Eskimo moved about with ease. How glad he was that he had come south!

In the meantime Aaka and Aapa moved from Barrow back to their old home in Wainwright. When a friend sent Patkotak a snapshot of his elderly parents standing in front of their sod igloo, that did it! A lump of homesickness fastened itself in his throat. Six years in the states had stacked up one on top of another too quickly.

"Now I want to go back to my dear old mother and dad," the young man announced with finality. "I want to see them again before they die."

With maturity the 25-year-old Patkotak cut loose his moorings, packed his few belongings and said good-bye to his friends in the downtown mission. They had been kind to him, but the needle on his compass pointed north. Then memory began replaying nearly-forgotten incidents of his trip

Saved

south. Patkotak, naive as they come. What a greenhorn! The Lord must have put three angels on duty just looking out for him.

Although still carrying a thick accent, Paul Patkotak's clear diction qualified him as an interpreter. William Van Valen, a village school teacher on his way back to Alaska to gather items of ethnological value, hired him. In his memoirs Van Valen described his enthusiastic young assistant as "a purebred Christian Eskimo boy."

Their ship docked at a quieter Nome than he remembered. Most of the prospectors and small-time operators had made it big, retired or left the country. While there, the pair rode several miles out of town to see the new mining operations. Huge hydraulic nozzles washed away dirt and gravel, getting down to bedrock as they sluiced for gold. Photographing scenes of interest for his employer, the returnee couldn't help but smile at himself—Paul Patkotak a tourist!

His heart almost skipped a beat when he spotted smoke far out over the sea. Could it be? Then the hull of his old acquaintance, "big smoke ship," took shape on the horizon. Drawing closer, the never-tiring cylinders that once throbbed, "Going south, going south," changed their tune.

Patkotak's ears picked up a new beat: "Going home, going home."

Every doubt vanished—he was headed home. This would be, however, his last trip on the Coast Guard cutter. In 1928 it was deemed "too old and too slow" for government service and put up for auction. Updating the weathered barkentine with a diesel engine, new owners sent it to Antarctica with personnel under the Byrd expedition. By the early 1950's, reports began leaking through of yet another worthy assignment for the *Bear.* Once more in its familiar groove as a mercy ship, it shuttled Jewish refugees across the Mediterranean Sea to Israel.

Back in Alaska, in 1919, as the two were about to leave Nome, Van Valen received word that he hadn't been approved for travel aboard the cutter. His plans aborted, the teacher authorized Patkotak to act as his agent by arranging for the purchase of artifacts at every stop. The young man enjoyed getting acquainted in villages along the way, but whenever the whistle blew prior to departure, he made it back on the double.

Weeks shrank into days, finally hours. Standing on deck, the excited traveler at last caught sight of the rising coastline south of Wainwright, then the village itself. "There are most of the houses like I remember them. Now I see people coming. I hope my parents got my letter...."

The couple was waiting for him. Though time had bent their frames and etched their countenances noticeably, they were still Aaka and Aapa. Sixth son had come home!

"As soon as I came back," Patkotak recalled, "I told my parents that I had met the Savior. I explained to them how He came into my heart with peace and happiness and how my fear of evil spirits melted away. Because I spoke their language, my parents could follow what I said. The missionaries who had to use interpreters or speak broken Eskimo weren't always easy to understand.

"Even though my family heard my words all right, I became like a stranger to them. My father was skeptical, but my mother listened with an open heart. She asked questions and thought about what I said. She was also very sick at that time and I was eager to help her in every way I could.

"After a while my mother opened up to me and told me of her inner struggles, the unrest and fear that followed her. She told me about her secret prayers. At last I was able to show her from the Bible the way to Jesus. She asked Him to come into her heart. How happy I was when God's love shined into my poor mother's soul!

"For a long time my dad never said anything. Then one day I said to my dad, 'Do you remember the time I was born? You wanted Aaka to put me into the snow because of no food in the village. Mom didn't say a word to you, Aapa. We have seen hard times, but I have something to tell you that has made me happy. I found Jesus, the Son of the living God. I want you to find Him too, like I found Him, the way the Bible says. I want you to go to Heaven like me, ready to meet the Lord.'

"I told my dad how to call on God. I said, 'Ask Him to have mercy on you a sinner, take the sin out of your heart like He did for me.'

"My dad prayed from his heart, crying, calling on God. God saved his soul like He saved mine. It made me happy.

"My dad said, 'I am ready to go like you, Sonny. I found Jesus too. You put a hunger in my heart to call on God even though I'm an old man eighty-some years old.'

"When my dad moved, he went on his hands and knees, he was so old. It made me praise God when he said he was ready to go when he died."

Saved

Patkotak got ahead of his story, skipping the two or three more years that his father lived. "Before my dad died, he had a dream or a vision. He said to me, 'Sonny, you told me from the Bible that Jesus said, "I am the way, the truth, and the life." The way is the trail.'

"He saw a trail, a straight and narrow path from earth to Heaven. That path was brighter than the lighted igloo. In the igloo we had a gasoline lamp and we used to think the gasoline light was the brightest light there was. It made me happy when my dad talked. He said he was going to follow the path—the trail from earth to Heaven. From that day on he never stopped talking about Jesus. The last time I looked at my Dad I saw something on his face. My tears started to run down and I know that some day I'll see him up in Heaven.

"Later on Mom went away to live with her grandchildren. They took her and cared for her when she was old. I wasn't there when she died, but she must have gone the same as my dad. I thank God that I came back home to see Mom and Dad again. I'm glad that I told them what Jesus did for me and He did the same for them."

Looking back, Patkotak chose to remember this brighter side of getting back into a familiar culture. One negative statement in reference to his

Alone in My Kayak

own people had nonetheless slipped out: "I became like a stranger to them."

During those years in another environment, the quiet teenager had grown into an outgoing adult. His peers found it hard to connect this strong person with the Patkotak they used to know. He had roamed far afield, and the smell of those fields clung to his garments. Never mind that, for it was just good to be back home. With a sigh of contentment he reached into the pot for a caribou bone, breaking it open to scrape out the rich marrow like he did as a boy. While he ate he answered the neighbors' questions. At first they wanted to hear all about the street cars on shiny tracks, powered by long poles reaching up to wires running the length of the city. And the beautiful church music—like the mouth harp they heard a sailor play, only lots more of it.

After they had heard enough, the young man kept on talking, probably telling more than his listeners wanted to hear. They looked at him askance: *What are you doing, Patkotak? Bragging? Telling us we've never seen anything?*

They weren't totally comfortable with mannerisms he had unconsciously picked up in the States either. Along with quoting his mission friends more often than deemed necessary, he spent a lot of time reading. His "store bought" clothes would have to go too. The list grew.

At first too happy to notice the sidelong glances shot his way, Patkotak finally had to concede that re-entry was not all he had fancied it to be.

"Many people looked at me uneasy," he reflected. "They thought I had come with crazy ideas, like maybe I wasn't telling the truth. They didn't want to hear everything I said. Then, too, it had become the thing to join the church even if you didn't know what it meant to live for the Lord. People tried to walk two directions at once. They got angry when I told them that Jesus could change their lives and save them from satan's power. Some of them went against me, but I made up my mind to pay no attention."

The young man might not have thought so at the time, but he did pay attention. Consistent cold shoulders were getting to him. Painfully groping to find his niche, the one who had slipped from favor began to withdraw from community activities. Rather than fighting back when slighted or ignored, he simply walked away—which didn't set so well either. *If that's the way you want it, Patkotak, it's all right by us.*

Should he have done more to bridge the gap between himself and his neighbors? If so, how?

There were other sincere Christians on the Arctic slope, but Paul Patkotak came across as a fanatic. It looked like a long lonely road ahead.

Chapter Ten

Home

Patkotak watched his mother as she shuffled slowly and painfully with hardly enough energy to carry out the simplest household tasks. One way or another he would make up for his years away from home.

Kignak's face lighted up when she talked with him about Heaven, but—like the rest of us—she still held this earthly life dear. Moreover, her last wishes remained unfulfilled. Their sod dwelling that afforded a snug shelter in winter felt dampish with melting snow seeping into the entrance. If only she and Alasurak could camp out far away

Alone in My Kayak

from the clutter that characterizes meager living. Aaka put her longings into words: "Before I die I want to go someplace where we can have sheep meat again. Nice, tender meat."

"Tender meat...." Her son understood. It almost hurt to look at her, realizing the price she paid to provide her growing family with warm waterproof footwear. Her teeth had been worn down to the gum from years of crimping the hard sealskin soles of dozens of pairs of *mukluks*.

"Go someplace...." He knew what that meant too. His mother was looking back to the years when they lived close to the mountains. They liked early autumn the best, when the Dall sheep clattered down to the lower crags and ravines to graze. What could be better than to feast once more on a tasty portion of sheep meat and drink its rich warm broth?

The hills of Kignak's youth lay far away, close to the northwest boundary of Canada. But whatever it took, he'd see her last wish come true. Acting on that decision, Patkotak moved his parents to Barrow as the first leg of their journey to sheep country. Hopefully, the following spring they could go on. In the meantime he hired out again to Van Valen so he could buy a dog team and other equipment for extended travel. Providing for his

Home

parents kept him busy six days a week; the seventh he claimed as his own. He attended church, but without opportunity to express himself. Maybe he should try to duplicate the mission services that had meant so much to him stateside—if he could find the right spot.

He found it, 12 miles from Barrow on the continent's northernmost point where approximately 15 families made their homes. Although ideally located for fishing, it was too far from the village proper for them to attend church on a regular basis. Getting permission to use one of the larger igloos, Patkotak arranged for his first service. Early Sunday morning he started walking. After a short distance he rested by dropping to his knees for prayer. This wasn't going to be as easy as he thought! After getting up, he went another few hundred yards before again sinking to his knees. Then once more ahead. He'd made a commitment and he'd follow it through.

In his own unsuspecting way, however, Paul Patkotak, who never claimed to be a preacher, failed to consider the possibility of his evangelistic outreach being misunderstood. The older missionaries who knew him had moved on and their replacements held misgivings about this fellow. Had he come to offer a substitute for the message of salvation proclaimed? They needed to find out.

Alone in My Kayak

Each week two or three elders followed him. When he entered one of the larger homes, they saw others living close by filter in until they crowded for space. Patkotak began by telling familiar Bible stories in Inupiaq, stories they could liken to their everyday lives. Heads nodded affirmation to what he said. "*Eee-Yah!* So that's how it was."

Spies leaning against the outer walls strained to listen. Without letting on that he heard footsteps or saw shadows against the sky light, the novice smiled with hidden pleasure as he raised his voice a few decibels. "Born again!" he shouted as he bore down on his subject. "You got to be born again, born of the Spirit. You got to give up everything if you want the best. And the best, that's Jesus!"

The eavesdroppers picked up nothing of a contrary nature to report to their leaders, for he only clarified what they had been trying to say all along. The outstanding difference in their messages was Patkotak's exuberance.

Should the new workers invite him to speak in the church? Those who knew him stood divided, the greater percentage unsure, for his fiery presentation hardly fit the norm. Another factor bore consideration as well. The local people might not be ready to accept one of their own as a leader.

Deep in their culture lay a concept of equality so strong that it frowned upon one rising above another even though it be for the common good. So, for reasons valid or otherwise, Brother Paul wasn't received. His meetings went on, but commitments to follow Christ were few. Patkotak remained a lone figure walking across the canvas, part of a picture without being really a part.

In Barrow, having lived some years there, the young man knew almost everyone. Hold it! Someone had come while he was away, a young woman working for the teachers. He later told about getting acquainted with this soft-spoken girl.

"In 1917 a man and his wife—her name was Ethel—came over from Canada. They had come to visit the husband's brother in Barrow. The man died leaving his wife, a Canadian Eskimo, with no relatives or friends.

"I went over to talk with her. She smoked a straw pipe and I asked her, 'Do you believe in Jesus?'

"She said, 'Yes.'

"I said, 'Do you want me to pray for you?' and she said, 'Yes.'

"I prayed for her. I asked the Lord to forgive her and take the sin out of her heart, take the sinful appetite away from her. She prayed too. Afterwards she said that she knew the Lord had saved her. I believed it. She said she can't smoke anymore, can't sing Eskimo worldly songs any more. The only desire she has is to pray. She remembered the time when she had taken some flour from people in Canada. She told me she would like to confess what she had stolen and ask forgiveness. She couldn't because they lived too far away.

"She had a hard time with no one to help her. I pitied her, and because I pitied her, I loved her. We got married and Ethel was a good help to me."

With their combined assets, they set up housekeeping. Ethel owned some cook pots and minimal camping equipment; Patkotak claimed a few things that had been his father's. What they lacked they would buy with his wages as guide and interpreter.

"That summer we didn't get any sheep," Patkotak recollected. "It's hard to find sheep close to Barrow. My parents lived until the following summer. We borrowed a boat and took them about 300 miles east to Barter Island where the mountains are nearer the coast and it's easier to hunt sheep."

They made the journey by dog-powered boat. To the bow Patkotak fastened a long rawhide tow

Home

line that reached to his team standing in harness on the shore. Though he could call commands to his lead dog, he frequently walked along the shore like the canal boat owners of old Europe with their horses. A dog can die from lapping salt water, so Patkotak carried fresh water, stopping frequently to give them a drink. Travel was slow and tedious except when a favorable wind encouraged them to hoist a caribou skin sail. Then the team frisked ahead at a steady pace.

The trip east, along a jagged coastline that added miles to their sea route, took several weeks. If their boat scraped bottom in shallow spots, they came to an abrupt stop. A hole in the *umiak*'s skin covering could spell costly delay. Quickly lengthening the tow line, they lifted and shoved the boat farther into the mainstream before proceeding on their way. Occasional stops broke the monotony of their journey—like when coming upon a small island no larger than a city lot where Arctic tern nested. These birds are among the most-traveled of all feathered creatures, flying back to Antarctica to spend the winter.

The couples stepped ashore ever so carefully, picked their way among drifted logs to find the baby birds, two to a nest, camouflaged in brown fuzzy down. Their white-feathered parents with red feet and bills circled wildly overhead, swooping down with angry screams at the intruders.

"Don't worry," the earth dwellers responded. "We're only trying to save your babies that got lost."

Sure enough, there would be a few nests with only one chick, the straggler a few feet away. If it was still alive, the fuzzy ball was put back beside his sibling. Most days, however, they kept moving until they reached a campsite at the mouth of a small river or stream. Patkotak built a fire right away. The old couple could poke the coals and add fuel while he bedded the dogs. Ethel dipped water into the big pot and prepared their evening meal. If they stopped at a lagoon where they could catch a few trout, they feasted on fresh fish over the fire. On clear nights the family slept out under the stars. If they chanced across an isolated home site or tent flapping in the wind, they were welcomed and begged to stay a while.

It took all four of them to answer the barrage of questions?

"Where did you camp last night?"

"How far have you come today?"

"Did you talk to our relatives before you left Barrow?"

"How's the hunting been?"

Later their hosts asked about the big world where Patkotak had been. The born storyteller fit neatly into the slot of actor-reporter as, with lighter vein, he re-enacted the fast pace of the Outside. He described massive buildings with marble steps, restaurants, libraries with rooms full of books. Would he like to go back? Someday maybe, but not to stay. Then again the story of his conversion— how God changed his life. He was a bearer of good news to those who had never heard it before. For the ones who had previous contact with the gospel, his words broke in like a ray of sunlight through an overcast sky. "We'll have a meeting, worship the Lord," Patkotak announced in his own forthright manner. Soon the entire group blended voices with his as they sang in their mother tongue. Sitting around the campfire, they saw the sun almost touch the horizon before it began its morning's ascent.

The trip eastward opened new vistas with names and locations Patkotak would visit in years to come: Cape Simpson, Beechey Point, Flaxman Island. He saw the little-known archipelago of mini-isles scattered in disarray along the coast. For the elderly parents, the slapping waves were fulfilling promises of reaching a long dreamed-of goal. The treeless terrain that had hardly changed since they last saw it held memories that only the listening heart can hear. They nodded their heads and smiled.

Sixth son liked to end the saga of their journey by adding, "At last my old mother had her desire more than filled. She wished to go someplace and she got to see the land she knew from a long time ago. She also had the finest tender sheep meat to eat day after day. I tell you that because it reminds me that our heavenly Father cares for us. He wants to give us good things right here on earth."

Near Barter Island the Patkotaks found an abandoned house that they were able to repair and move into before winter storms set in. The parents stayed with them until Alasurak passed away. After burying him at Anderson Point, they took Kignak back to Barrow to live with other relatives. Once more the young couple made the long journey back to the Beaufort Sea region to establish permanent residence.

Paul Patkotak had found the right companion in gentle Ethel. Having worked for school teachers, she could appreciate his tastes that occasionally asked for "white man's food." She was also a crack show with her rifle. With their give-and-take relationship, the Patkotaks were able to share in almost every aspect of living. Defying a culture that emphasized separation of men's and women's

Home

chores, their teamwork put up a double front against the tough demands of the Arctic.

"When my wife and I were young, we used to like to hunt together," Patkotak said. "We loaded up the sled, hooked up our dogs and started out. One time we traveled a long way toward the mountains. We came to a good place to set up our tent on a flat piece of ground. My wife stayed in the tent as she had just given birth to our first child, Olive, on August seventh. My wife had to look after her.

"That time when sheep hunting, I had a very special happening. I headed out to find wild meat. After a long hike, I spotted a big ram far back in the mountains. I came upon it by walking a long way around so it wouldn't see me. After I shot the animal, I took out the insides. Just the same the ram weighed between 80 and 100 pounds. I would have to carry it about 12 miles to our tent.

"I knew it wouldn't be easy to hike long ways with a sheep on my back. Anyway, I was thankful for a good hunt. We are always thankful, for we know what it means to have little meat in the pot."

Picking his way down the mountainside, Patkotak soon got too warm. With each step the pack on his back felt heavier. He stumbled. Careful lest his feet slip under the load, he lifted the sheep off his back and lay down to rest.

Alone in My Kayak

"Praise You, Lord," the tired man breathed from the depths of his heart. "My wife and I shall have a good evening meal when I come in with this. Thank You, for taking care of us."

While basking in the sunshine, something caught his attention. "I saw the cloud turning, going around, a kind of whirlwind," he described with excited recall. "It took the form of a great whirly ball as it came closer, like it was following in my tracks. I began to get uneasy. For safety's sake I put the sheep on my back again and braced myself against the whirlwind as it came closer. When it reached me, I could feel that it touched only the animal on my back. I fought against it. I wasn't going to give up my meat!

"I tried hard, but the whirlwind loosened my hold. I couldn't hang on any more. I could feel it lift the sheep up over my head. There it was, the carcass in front of me, carried upright in the whirlwind. That was something to see! I ran after it shouting. At last I gave up, watching as it traced the path I had taken that morning on my way to the mountains.

"Then I began to understand what was taking place. I remembered that the Lord had promised to take care of me, so I needn't be afraid. He who gave me the meat would see to it that I got home to my wife with it.

" 'Hallelujah!' I shouted. 'It's the Lord! Thank You, Jesus, for helping me!'

"The wind carried the sheep swiftly and safely, and I hurried after. As I looked far over the land, I saw the whirlwind set the ram down by our tent. Then the whirlwind disappeared.

"I ran all the way home. My wife was in the tent and never saw what happened. I called to her, 'If you had been outside the tent, you would have seen a miracle. The Lord sent a whirlwind that carried my sheep all the way home. Come and see it. The Lord is in the wind.' "

Patkotak related another incident that happened shortly afterward, one that could so easily have ended in tragedy.

"We got seven dogs so we could go trapping. I had some seal meat for our dogs and some grub for ourselves—my wife and I and our first daughter who was not a year old at the time. It was a long ways east of Barrow where we were going to trap white fox. When we got to the place, we found a sod igloo someone had made many years before. We made up our minds to stay in it. While we were there, we got short of food for ourselves, and especially for our dogs. I said, 'Soon we will have no dog food. We will have to go back 75 miles for food.'

Alone in My Kayak

"In the morning we have morning worship up there. We had only one rifle. After we had worship-time, I heard a still small voice above my head say, 'Paul, you had better leave your rifle home. You go to the trap line without it today. Leave your rifle for your wife.'

"I figured, 'No. My dad always told me not to leave my rifle home.'

"Again it said, 'Something will come today.' It didn't say what will happen. It only said 'Something will come today.'

"I looked at my wife. She didn't seem to hear anything. After a while I said to my wife. 'The Spirit of God said to me, 'You better leave the rifle home. Something will come today to our camp here.' I had better leave my rifle for you. I will go on without it.'

"Whenever I leave with my dogs I usually don't come home until evening. My wife helped me to hitch up the dogs, leaving the little baby inside in the cradle. When I was ready I shouted. 'Mush!' and the dogs started to run.

"After I had gone about ten minutes or longer, again I heard a voice above my head, 'Paul, turn back quick! Quick!'

Home

"I put my foot on the brake of my sled to stop my dogs. I yelled, 'Come, haw!' which means, 'Come back, turn back!' Again I called to the leader, 'Come, haw!'

"They turned around right away, for dogs always run fast when they are going home.

"There was an old rack by our igloo. Someone had left old skins hanging there. As I was nearing home I saw right away something had happened. The rack was torn down and scattered on the snow. When I got there my wife was slow coming out of the igloo. That was unusual too as she usually comes out quick when she hears the sound of dogs. It made me wonder when I saw cartridges in front of the entrance to the igloo and no cover on the rifle. The first thing I thought was that a polar bear had attacked, maybe eaten her and our baby too!

"Finally my wife came out. She said, '*Arrah nunoot*,' meaning 'Something happened, too much bother.'

"What?" I asked before she finished. "Where are they?"

"My wife answered. 'Two polar bears out there dead.'

" 'Two?'

Apparently shaken by the experience, Ethel summed up her brief encounter with, "I shot twice and that was enough."

Alone in My Kayak

"When my wife was a little girl in Canada," Paul Patkotak went on to explain, "her father gave her a rifle and she practiced shooting squirrels. She was a perfect shooter. After she helped me unharness the dogs and tie them up by the chain, I went down to see the polar bears. When I got to the place, I thanked God. I couldn't keep still. I kept saying, 'Praise God! Praise God!'

"We froze lots of meat, a big bear and a big cub. My wife told me she was cutting up our last meat that morning when she heard our little puppy tied up in the hallway bark. As soon as Ethel went outside she saw these two polar bears right by the rack chewing something.

"She turned back, got the rifle, knelt down on the snow and aimed. Only one shot and the bear turned away, walking slowly to the sand where it dropped down dead. The cub was licking up the blood of the big one—that's the way they do. While it was doing that, my wife got on top of the igloo. She needed to get a little higher. With that second shot she dropped the cub on top of the mother.

"We didn't have to go to Barrow to get food for ourselves or dog food either. Besides that, the polar bear skins were worth quite a bit. Something else good. Down by the lake lived an old couple who had nothing to eat but fish all winter. We gave them meat too.

"My God is real. He has done so much for me and when I needed Him most He never failed me."

Chapter Eleven

Family

From a practical standpoint, Paul and Ethel Patkotak made a wise choice by moving into the Beaufort Sea region with its unclaimed territory for traplines. The location provided easy access to the mountains as well to the open sea. Their house was built of sizeable drift logs with earth packed solidly against the lower walls for added insulation. By repairing and updating the abandoned dwelling, they had a cozy home that never trembled under winter storms.

Patkotak's knowledge of the value of a dollar helped him bargain with furs and ivory carvings in exchange for foodstuff and ammunition. During the short summer months he met trading vessels on their way to Canada; in winter he dog-teamed or snowshoed to Tom Gordon's Store on Barter Island.

With their semi-nomadic background, the family was proficient in the art of sled travel. If for some reason Ethel hesitated to take the children on an outing, Patkotak went alone. Northern hospitality allowed added hours for visiting neighbors of miles away. When met with an overnight delay, he asked for the privilege of reading his Bible and, true to pattern, expounded on it. Though not a theological giant, his homespun illustrations drove basic truths straight home.

Moreover, neighbors agreed, it looked as if the Lord really did look out for the Patkotaks. According to the standards of their time, the family fared well. They worked hard, yet found time for summer camping. Neither did Patkotak lack for means of transportation. While a man of less means might have had to count on his own physical strength for hauling supplies, he had a boat for summer use as well as a string of well-fed sled dogs. He was content with his modest success, taking the word "prosper" in his well-worn King James Bible to mean needs met with something left over to give to others. Looking back, one of their sons commented, "We always shared food, gave meat. It was good and it was right."

Of their home a daughter added, "From living with the teachers my mother learned many things about keeping house. We were never hungry either. My father was a great hunter and he traded skins for food. I remember him coming home with sacks of four, a keg of butter kept in brine and cases of canned milk."

Their father home schooled, teaching his offspring the three R's. He told them the time-worn stories of their people too, but drew the line on those packed with fear. Why carry on the grim warning about northern lights that played across their winter sky?

"Don't talk loud about them," his own parents had cautioned with an ominous tone that implied more than their words said. "If they hear you, they might come down. And if they ever touch us, they'll kill us."

Patkotak chose to give his children a healthy view of the fantastic ribbons that whirled in rhythm, then hung in gorgeous silence before suddenly taking off on another dance.

"Come and look at those northern lights, even prettier than last night. See? God put those lights

Alone in My Kayak

in the sky. In winter when everything's white we need pretty colors to make us happy, so He gives those lights."

When a younger child clapped her hands to see if she could make the lights move faster, the others laughed. Family fun. Going back indoors and shutting the heavy door against the penetrating cold, the father sat down by the fire. With the littlest one dandled on his knees and the others pushing tightly against him, he told stories—most of which they had heard before, but the best always bore repeating.

Besides friendly contacts that the Patkotaks initiated, distant neighbors occasionally dropped by to see them. One day a man searching for grazing land for reindeer herds knocked at their door. Within minutes they found themselves on common ground, for their visitor also knew the Lord. Suddenly Paul and Ethel Patkotak realized how much they needed fellowship with other believers. They'd gone so long without....

A couple of days later several more herders appeared, setting up their conical tents nearby. These Laplanders had emigrated from northern Scandinavia to tend reindeer and pass their skills on to the Eskimo. The Patkotak children looked wide-eyed at the men with their easy, comfortable

Family

manners. Clothed mostly in furs, their latest Lap fashions (especially their turned-up-toe boots) fascinated the girls who right away wanted their mother to copy the trim and tassels for their own boots and mittens.

Billy and Steven studied the men so unlike anyone they had ever met. "If they have hundreds of reindeer," the boys reasoned, "why do they just stand and watch them? If those were ours, we'd kill them and have a feast."

"No," their father replied, "you wouldn't. Those men are like the Christmas shepherds in the Bible who took from their flocks only when they needed to. Their animals provide them with meat and skins, with milk too. The first milk I had came from a mother caribou which is almost the same as a reindeer."

"What did the milk taste like?"

"I don't remember. I was too little."

The family liked to thumb through these memories. It goes without saying that they faced hardships too—like the miserable winter the children came down with whooping cough. The parents took turns walking the floor with the first one and then another. What a relief when the last child recovered with no serious aftereffects!

Their happiness, however, was cut short when Mary, who could keep the family entertained with her charming two-year-old antics, got a fever. Though Patkotak and Ethel prayed, her temperature rose higher. Her chubby cheeks lost their color. One day it was over. Ethel placed her, their second daughter, in a small chest Patkotak made. He carried the burden out to Anderson Point where they dug a shallow grave. Perhaps they'd find a bit of consolation by laying her close to Aapa who had died some years before.

What took the child? Who knows from back in those days of no doctors or medical facilities? The family seldom referred to Mary's brief chapter. Better to turn the page and go on.

On an everyday basis the couple felt comfortable within their set boundaries. Then gradually the very limitations that promised security began to gnaw at them. Perhaps their freedom had outlived its day. Their children too—Olive, Steven, Billy, and now Simeon and Elizabeth—were missing out on friendships important to their growing-up years.

One day Patkotak went out alone. When he failed to return after several hours, Ethel sent the two older boys to look for him. Maybe he had an accident and needed help. Walking along the

Family

beach where their father often went to get driftwood, the boys found him lying face down between a couple of logs. They stopped. Drawing closer, they heard him praying. After looking long enough for the sacred scene to print itself indelibly on their minds, they turned away from their father's trysting place, his driftwood altar where he prayed for family and friends. He prayed there for churches, for revival to sweep across the north and for the Lord's will to be done in his own life. Now the time had come for him to put action to those prayers. As head of the family he must face the issue squarely: A life of continued withdrawal smacked of selfishness.

He had to admit that the children's education lacked. They needed fresh challenges along with the give-and-take of group participation. It was time to get back into the mainstream of society. Another decision followed: choosing the right village. Families vacating their remote campsites had more than doubled Barrow's population. With parents no longer losing an alarming number of their offspring, the school there rollicked with youngsters. Although easier to keep clean, the small frame houses rapidly replacing the old sod igloos had their disadvantages too. Most of them were poorly insulated, inviting winter's wind to whistle through the seams. To make matters

Alone in My Kayak

worse, driftwood had become increasingly hard to find, and imported fuel was costly.

All these factors considered, Patkotak opted to return to Wainwright. Within days after moving to their home village, the five children got acquainted with other youngsters, later trudging off to school with them like one extended family. Their father was able to supply necessities so the Patkotaks, as yet not tantalized by modern frills, lived happily within their means. Then the terrible pinch. Though the Alaskan Arctic hadn't fully emerged into a cash society, World War II left an impact that resembled the Great Depression of the 30's. The coined phrase "hard times" fit into their vocabulary distressingly well. The fur market hit an all-time low, the price of a fox skin dropping to a dollar—with no buyers either. Trading vessels, their former contact with the rest of the world, had been conscripted for military service. At least rationing wasn't an annoyance—sugar and other staples simply weren't to be had. Cupboards stood bare. A bleak terrain never designed to accommodate a burgeoning population balked.

His best intentions notwithstanding, Patkotak had to take his children from school to go hunting with him. Inasmuch as the dogs weren't able to haul camping equipment and the family too, the older children started walking a couple hours

Family

before the team's departure. Granted, it was dangerous, but what else could they do? When the team caught up with the first contingent, they took a lunch break. Then it was the team's turn to trot on ahead of those who walked. A couple of hours later the parents stopped to set up camp.

"Are the children coming yet?" Ethel would ask, fearing lest those following some distance behind might meet a bear or somehow lose their way.

Patkotak, on constant lookout, stalled his answer until he thought he saw a far-off speck moving in their direction. "I think...yes, I think I see them," he ventured.

Straining his eyes against the fading sunlight, he at last confirmed with sureness, "I do see them. Yes, I do. Walking slow, but steady. Everything's all right."

What a relief to finally set up camp again! When the family managed to get meat to last them a few weeks, they returned to the village to put the children back in school. In church too. Though Paul Patkotak never applied for membership in the local body, he attended regularly. He was always quick to give credit to its early missionaries who had introduced him to the wonders of the printed page. They had laid the foundation for his faith, for which he would be forever grateful.

Alone in My Kayak

On Saturdays the youngsters brought in fuel and water to tide the household over until Monday. After a time of play they settled down by lamplight to review the week's Scripture memory verses. The family wasn't to be embarrassed if one of them was called upon for their memorization in Sunday school. Admittedly the youngsters rated Sunday as the most boring day of the week, but they weren't alone in this. Proper communities of that era, whether north or south, had their share of blue laws which the average citizen felt compelled to observe. Enjoy or endure—take your pick.

Then something happened to throw a new light on keeping the Lord's Day. During the winter when cash flow hit bottom, hunting also struck a new low as ice formed thick and solid over the sea. Families living for weeks on nothing but small river smelt dared not be unthankful—not with stories of the winter of 1891 resurfacing. At least Patkotak knew where to release pent-up fears.

"Lord, increase my faith," he prayed. "I want to believe, to lay hold of Your promises. Help me be like David who said that he had never seen the righteous forsaken nor his seed begging bread. We might go through hard places, but still our trust is in You."

It happened on a Sunday morning when he opened the door and stepped out. He could scarcely believe his eyes. Open water! His heart leaped—meat! The next instant his heart sank—Sunday!

Family

How could he think of tearing down his godly testimony by going hunting?

With childlike simplicity he dropped to his knees and prayed aloud: "Lord, You know that I won't go hunting today just for the fun of hunting. This is Your day, but my family is hungry and I must provide for them. So forgive me that I go out."

Late that afternoon the father returned with two seals. Gathered around the table, the family laughed as they ate. It had been years since anything tasted so good. Even though every hunter in the village undoubtedly went out on the ice that day, Patkotak worried that he might be the cause of someone stumbling over the liberty he had taken. Come mid-week service, he walked determinedly over to the church to clear his slate.

The conscientious believer asked for the privilege of saying a few words before the Bible lesson. When his turn came, he stood to his feet to explain why he'd gone hunting. If his so doing offended them, would they please forgive him? Whether those present accepted his confession or shrugged it off as being totally irrelevant made no difference to him. He had delivered his soul.

What Patkotak didn't know was that someone sat tall as he listened to a man admitting his

Alone in My Kayak

doubts about himself. "My dad," the boy thought proudly. "That's my dad."

The children remember their father as being generous with his time. Wanting his sons to grow up feeling secure and self-reliant, he passed on skills that had been handed down to him. At the same time Ethel taught the girls. If stitches weren't even, the learner took them out and started over. Every year before Christmas the entire family had to be outfitted with new clothes. While the mother fashioned fine parkas and warm boots, their oldest child Olive made their lighter weight garments.

One morning while the family was staying in a hunting site some distance from Wainwright, Olive got up early to sew. Suddenly she heard the crunch of heavy feet breaking through the crusted snow. Who could it be? Her father and Steven were out hunting. The unfamiliar sound sent shivers racing up her spine.

Slipping quickly to her mother's bedside, she whispered, "Aaka, Aaka, someone or something is outside our door!"

Cautiously Ethel peered out the window. As her eyes became accustomed to winter's dim light, she spotted a huge polar bear dragging meat down from their rack! Ethel would rather leave the big game for Patkotak and Steven, but she had to do

Family

something. A wild animal was about to devour their food supply. What if it afterwards broke into their house?

Without a sound Ethel lifted down an old 300 Savage rifle from the wall. Handling a smaller rifle to her son Billy, she gave careful instruction. "If I miss, you're ready and you fire."

The teenager crouched low beside his mother as she stealthily opened the door barely wide enough for the barrel. He didn't get his big chance. Aiming at her target, his mother shot. Right on!

"The bear toppled over dead, but my mother didn't go out," the youngest daughter Elizabeth commented. "She waited for my dad to come and take care of the meat."

In spite of lean winters, the family made it through until the war ended. With the return of trade, the economy took an upswing. That meant staying home, going to school and attending church as before.

"Good times," people said. "Yes," the Patkotaks could reply. "Yes, but...."

Ethel was beginning to complain of feeling tired; light household chores became too much for her. Patkotak watched his wife anxiously when she coughed. The disease that had already taken

Alone in My Kayak

many of their people had moved into her lungs. Tuberculosis. Hoping that his companion would benefit by staying inland where they could escape the merciless winds that buffeted their coast, he once more moved his family back out to a camp. They would work together as one to do whatever was best for Mother. With plenty of rest and an unwavering trust in God, she'd make it through.

Just as they expected, Ethel rallied. To further buoy their faith, no one else was tainted by her sickness.

As daylight lengthened, Patkotak watched for the first flock of migratory birds winging northward. Springtime. They could go back to Wainwright again.

Olive and Steven were by then working and on their own. Billy was away at boarding school. Elizabeth and Simeon, who still lived at home, helped load the big sled. Having done it before, they knew how to place each item of size for balance. Afterward they fit household goods, food and clothing into hollows and crannies, leaving the best spot for Mother who would ride all the way.

It was travel as usual until the dogs that had pulled at a somewhat steady pace with their weighty load suddenly yelped wildly. They had

Family

spotted a fox out on the ice! Lunging forward for the chase, the foolish animals jerked the sled. Ethel, caught off guard, lost her balance. The too-sharp turn that threw her out twisted the sled at an angle, dealing her a second cruel blow as she landed with a sickening thud on the hard-packed snow. The accident left her with a back injury and serious damage to her already weakened lungs.

At home in Wainwright, Ethel grew weaker. This time the family's prayers weren't being answered in the way that they had hoped. Did God want to take His precious child to Himself? No question that she wanted to go.

Simeon looked back at her last days on earth. "We stood by her bed and watched her. My sister Elizabeth and I cried because we knew we were losing our mother. Suddenly she looked up, just like she was seeing something.

" 'Don't cry, Simeon and Elizabeth,' she said, 'What I'm looking at right now is a glorious place. No sadness in the place where I'm going.'

"I'm sure the Lord reveals things to people when they are going. I know that my mother saw something wonderful. She was happy, but I turned away. I couldn't stay any longer and I wasn't there when she died a few hours later. I didn't go to her funeral either. I was only about 12 or 13 years old and to me it was a real loss."

Alone in My Kayak

Ethel slipped away from this world May 8, 1944, leaving Patkotak as a single parent with full responsibility for keeping the home. The widower's heart ached for Simeon who pulled into his shell, keeping his emotions so hidden that no one could touch them. Because Elizabeth often stayed with her sister Olive, who filled the role of second mother to her, she didn't feel her loss as keenly. Slowly, however, the realization of an empty place crept in. The secondary hurt wasn't easy to take either.

"We'll hang in there together," the father thought. In whatever way he could, he'd give his children the best of his time, sharing what he himself treasured most.

"Our dad read to us every morning," they recalled. "He read from the Bible—Ezekiel, Jeremiah, Revelation. He read it all to us. He read from the King James Version and translated into Eskimo as that was the language we used in our home. He never preached to us. He never pointed a finger and said, 'You do this or that.' Instead he would tell stories about what he had seen.

" 'The man who respects Sunday, he gets blessed,' he would say. Then he would tell about when he went out with a whaling captain that got a whale every year. 'Six days are enough,' the captain would say. Every year he got a whale even when hunting wasn't good.

Family

"He talked to us about authority too. He told us that the man who tries to follow what the leaders say, he will live long. Something always happens to those who make it hard for others. I used to see a lot of people make fun of him, but my father lived what he said."

The children felt the brunt of criticism directed against their father. "Sometimes our schoolmates accused him of being too religious," one of them added. "When they mocked us I took it quite hard. I thought it was dumb of father to be so different, but today I thank God for him."

During those in-between years when the young people were trying to find themselves, they seemed to shed their father's instruction like water off an oiled tarp. Where had he gone wrong? Sugarcoated discipline—was that it? Had his own hurts blinded him to their more immediate needs? Patkotak pondered the proverb, "Train up a child in the way he should go: and when he is old, he will not depart from it" (Prov. 22:6). His children departed. Or did they?

One day one of his sons entered a store where older men grouped around the stove to enjoy their tobacco and exchange village tidbits. The 19-year-old who just came in didn't walk in his father's footsteps, so how about a laugh? They began

Alone in My Kayak

ridiculing Patkotak's religion, expecting this youth to add a bit of spice to their wisecracks. Their listener, not responding as they had expected, glared back at them with scorn. Who were these Saturday-for-the-world, Sunday-for-the-church, Monday-for-themselves fellows to belittle his dad? They had their nerve, making fun of him. His old man might be kind of odd in some ways, but he was honest—which was more than he could say for them.

"Hypocrites!" he yelled in open, defiant anger. "That's what you are. Hypocrites!"

The mockers cringed, not drawing an easy breath until he had slammed the door behind him. Defeated and chagrined, they looked shamefacedly at one another. In spite of his apparent rebellion, this son knew what Christianity was all about. His father had instilled basic principles in his children from which they could never get away.

Patkotak, who knew nothing of the incident, floundered in the pits of discouragement. In his aloneness he longed for a human touch. Ethel was gone. His children were leaving the nest, ready to try their own wings. Who would stand by him now? Anyone at all, Lord? Like the prophet Elijah, Patkotak voiced his complaint, "I, only I, am left."

He had tried to walk with God, but what was the use? No one cared. The next question followed automatically. "Does God care?"

Family

In spite of this down period in his life, the stalwart Christian couldn't deny his faith. He had always placed top priority on the written Word for finding answers to life's perplexing questions. He wasn't known as a visionary, which in turn gave credence to this one dream that held special meaning for him. In it he saw a number of his acquaintances and above each of them glowed a small light. Over one in particular, Michael Kayutak, he saw a brighter, steadier flame. When he awoke he interpreted the dream to be a reminder to him that, regardless of minor doctrinal differences, every born again believer has received the light of life. Alone as he felt, he accepted correction: *Get this straight, Patkotak, you aren't the only true follower.*

The larger, steadier flame over Kayutak? It seemed as if the Lord had let him know that there was one who related to spiritual truths more than he was given credit for. Furthermore, he had a capacity to listen, to empathize, when Patkotak needed a shoulder to lean on. Whether or not Kayutak held views in total agreement with his or chose the same exacting life style wasn't of prime importance. He had one priceless quality—loyalty—found only in a friend who knows how to stand by. Moreover, who's to say that a comrade through thick and thin isn't a gift from God?

Chapter Twelve

Provision

If anyone talked too much about going back to the ways of their forefathers, Patkotak and his peers could remain obviously silent. They remembered the hardships that went along with "the good old days," hunger that meant more than whetted appetite, famine that reduced the best hunters to groping for anything to keep them alive. They'd seen enough of fevers and infections, of broken bones not set properly.

"We didn't know any better," one woman confided. "When my brother accidentally shot himself, we took our *ulus* and trimmed the torn flesh.

Later the doctor told us he couldn't do much because we had cut away muscles too. That's why his arm hangs useless. We just didn't know...."

The injured man lived, but he dragged along a heavy price tag. Nor did it help to know that they weren't the only ones to make such a mistake. In the previous century European doctors had also cut tendons in an effort to straighten drawn limbs. Now the world was looking to modern technology for help, and our native peoples would likewise reap its benefits.

At the same time many shuddered at the waste of natural resources shown by non-natives moving into the region. Others chose to follow an easier route, disregarding the accumulated knowledge the Inuit had handed down to their children and children's children. That which held continuing value they must keep, but at the same time they let some of their traditions and superstitions go. Like a living language, their culture had to be allowed to reshape itself as the need arose. Stagnated, it would lose its effectiveness.

So it was that Patkotak surprised a group of visitors who complimented him on his handsome parka. "Did you trap those furs yourself?" they asked.

"No," came his matter-of-fact reply. "This I bought my last trip to Seattle. I walked by a store.

Provision

Fur coats for sale. I went in and looked around. I saw this fine coat, a woman's coat, and I tried it on. It fit good, but it was way too long. Anyway, I said, 'I'll take it.'

"The ladies working there looked at me funny and smiled a bit. Smiled like they were thinking that old man doesn't know what he wants. But I know what I want. When I came home, I cut off the bottom and used that part to make a parka hood. I know how to sew skins and my daughter helped me. She made a real Eskimo band for it and I got a good parka cheap. Not much work to it either. Our heavenly Father provides in many ways."

We can't be too proud to accept His gifts because they might be different, and we can't be too independent to call for help either, Patkotak emphasized. With that he told a more exciting story that took place a long way from the fur shops of the lower 48. Once more he was back on the north slope hunting.

"My wife and I went to the mountains, the Brooks Range near Barter Island, sledding with my dog team. Then I left the team and climbed higher up by myself. High up there on the top of the mountain I slipped and started to fall down the side of the mountain. I was rolling faster and faster and couldn't stop. When I tried to look down at the bottom, I couldn't see land, it was so steep.

"I got really scared, then I remembered to call on God from my heart. 'God stop me!' I hollered.

"I stopped right there at that very moment that I called on God to stop me. Like a magnet holding something, that was me. I was hanging to the rock that stuck out, held by my two hands and my toes.

"I tried the rocks first to see if they were solid enough to hold me, which they were. At the same time tears were running down from my eyes and I was praising the Lord for answering my call. I started climbing back up the mountain until I got to a place where I could stand up without using my hands.

"Then I lifted my hands in the air and shouted, 'Praise Jesus for saving my life again.!'

"I kept climbing until I got to where I could walk. I still had my rifle on my back, tied to my body. I went home without getting anything, but with victory in my soul. That is most important, always victory in my soul. God showed me again that He takes care of His children. I never got anything, but I went back the next day and never gave up hunting."

Like anyone else, Patkotak liked to come out on top, yet he frankly admitted to being to blame for some of his worst moments. With typical candor the veteran told about another near-disaster when he was out hunting alone. His aim wasn't right on that particular day when he shot a bearded seal weighing close to 700 pounds. Mistake number one: He didn't realize that he had barely wounded the *ugruk*, which meant one hurt, angry creature in powerful resistance. Mistake number two: When he threw out a hook that embedded itself in his prey, he gave the line too much slack. Before he could correct the situation, the rope had wrapped itself around his outer parka. With a burst of mean strength the injured *ugruk* streaked for open water, tightening the line and dragging the hunter with it. Struggling to keep his footing, the captor taken captive sprang from one ice cake to another. He hopscotched until exhausted, knowing that each skip was taking him closer to open water. A slight misstep meant the bottom of the sea. Patkotak tugged frantically at the taut line, hoping to ease it enough to free himself. No way! If only the animal would pause long enough for him to reach for his knife, he could cut the line. Finally coming to his senses, Patkotak expanded his burning lungs with a desperate cry: "Lord, help me! Save me!"

Instantly the *ugruk* stopped, its huge body slowly surfacing without a twinge. Release for both man and beast. Between short breaths, the hunter with deep emotion thanked God for another deliverance. After freeing himself he threw the line over his shoulder and began the long trek back to shore. Pulling the *ugruk* along behind him, he stepped carefully from one ice floe to the next until he reached shore ice and safety. Home at last, tuckered out and triumphant—yet humbled.

This episode reminded him of another that to some might border on the unbelievable.

"One time I was going out on a caribou hunt," he began. "That was back in the early 40's. My blood cousin who wasn't a born again Christian wanted to go with me. I wanted him to go with me too. It was October and we traveled about two days over hard tundra. It was good hunting and we each had 17 caribou. When it was time for us to go back to Wainwright, we couldn't take all our meat with us. No room in our sleds.

"My cousin worried. 'Look' he said, 'here are tracks all around us. We can't just leave our meat for the wolves and the wolverines. We will have to build a solid ice house for storing our meat.' "

As an alternative, they could encase their kill by repeatedly covering it with snow, then pouring on water to form layers of ice. Maybe a wolf doesn't know how to get through the hard glass-like

Provision

mound, but the wolverine does. With criminal intent the scamp lies down to let its body heat melt a spot of ice. After clawing away the soft ice, it lies down again. By repeating this tedious little maneuver, the thief gets to the meat and eats or destroys as suits him best. In the end not one scrap remains for the rightful owners.

Patkotak continued their discussion. " 'No,' I said, 'I'm not going to cut ice or make ice either. I will cover my meat with snow. After I cover it up, I am going to pray for the Lord to keep it safe. I didn't kill caribou for the animals. I killed caribou for my children to eat.'

"I covered the carcasses with soft snow just like I said. Afterwards I prayed and asked God to take care of my meat for me and my family. 'Don't let wolves or wolverines disturb my meat,' I prayed. 'Don't let them touch what belongs to my family.'

"My cousin just stared at me without saying a word. I don't know all that went through his mind, but I saw what he looked like. Like he was thinking, 'You are more foolish than I thought!'

"I packed as much meat as I could find for in my sled. I said, 'Lord, I'm counting on You to watch the meat till I get back. Thank You, Lord. Amen.'

"Just the same, when my cousin saw what I did, he copied me. He left a big heap of meat covered with a bit of snow. But he forgot the most important part. He didn't ask God to watch over it and he didn't thank Him either. He didn't pray because he was still a man of the world.

"So we started out, happy that we could go home with so much. Then something we never counted on came up—a warm wind coming from the southwest. The river that was solid ice when we came over was now cracked up on the edges and the water came up in the center. It does that every time when warm weather comes. The river was wide because we were near its mouth, near to the sea.

"As we were going long, my cousin was leading. He hollered at me that we must turn back.

" 'Water in front of us, straight through. What will we do? Shall we go up over the land?'

" 'We better not move up that way,' I answered him. 'The land is rough, and the sleds are too heavy with meat.' "

Compared to present-day sled dogs bred for racing, these heavy-chested canines looked like draft horses. Leaders were chosen for intelligence and obedience, the rest of the team for pulling power. Nine well-cared-for dogs averaged 40 miles in a day easily. But with their day nearly done, the men couldn't risk a long strenuous route home.

Provision

"I had to put my rope on, like a harness," Patkotak further explained. "Many times we have to help pull the sled, especially when the snow gets soft. It wasn't easy. I heard my cousin holler again, 'Water! No way except straight across water. What will we do?'

" 'I will go right toward the middle of the river on the ice,' I called back to him. 'If you want to, you can take the long way over land. But you don't need to. We can go right on like we planned.'

"Although the water was open out there ahead of us, I kept my mind on the Lord. I cried from my heart for Him to make the way for us. At the same time I remembered Moses and the Red Sea. I didn't look at the water. I looked down, moving along very slowly with my mind on the Lord. When we stopped, I looked up. I saw right ahead of us, water on both sides with a narrow opening. Solid ice—just enough to get through with our sleds.

"I told my cousin to keep going and we started to move faster. In front of us an open path, and behind us the water came together again. After we had passed the dangerous part my heart felt like it wanted to burst, I was so grateful. We made it safe across. Nothing to do but to stop and praise God.

"My cousin watched me walk back and forth, my hands in the air, shouting, 'Thank You, Jesus!

Alone in My Kayak

Thank You, Jesus!' many times. We see it again that the Lord answers our prayers.

"My cousin stood to one side with tears flowing down his face. 'Patkotak,' he finally said, 'Now I know that your God is real.' Just before we continued our journey home, he added, 'I will also be a Christian like you. Soon.'

"Later, when it was time for us to go and pick up the rest of our meat, I took my whole family along because it was nice weather. Almost springtime by then. When we reached high ground where we could look ahead and see our store of caribou, we knew there had been visitors. As we got closer we saw that my cousin's supply was gone. Mine lay untouched even though wolves had left tracks all around it. The Lord had watched my food supply just as I had asked Him to. Praise His name!

"My poor cousin still hadn't lived up to his promise to become a Christian. Now he was once more being reminded of how great our God is. I looked at him with pity. He had nothing to feed his nine dogs, so I gave of my supply. After we got home we divided the rest between us.

"You can be sure I believe in miracles. I believe in the God who has all power in Heaven and in

Provision

earth. For Him nothing is impossible. My God is real."

Several years later Patkotak's cousin did surrender his life to the Lord. Even before then, if someone expressed doubt about the authenticity of this particular account, Oliver calmly affirmed, "I was there."

Like any wise hunter Patkotak made it a practice to travel over safe ice. This once-in-a-lifetime miracle took place of necessity. At the same time it confirmed to them God's willing involvement in their daily lives.

In his later years, Patkotak continued to see the Lord's provision, though not always with breathtaking action. Hard work and long hours with his team had taken its toll on his physical strength. He became more appreciative of one of Wainwright's special advantages—fuel for the taking within walking distance of his house.

"In my home village," he explained, "we have coal, lignite, but it's not always easily come by. In the summer after the ice goes away, the wind starts to blow from the southwest. When the wind dies down we walk on the beach where we see tons of coal, washed up from the bottom of the ocean, lying on the sand. Sometimes we also find ivory fossil tusks, beautiful color, good for carving. All we have to do is sack up the coal for winter. Every time I picked up coal I thanked God for the coal and for the mussels that hang on it. I know God sends us these good things.

"In the fall of the year a big blow starts. One time when the storm was over I walked about two miles away along the beach. I saw lots of coal. Other people went down too, sacked coal and backpacked it to the top of the bluff. I put mine on the sand because I didn't want to work so hard and tire my body. Then I went home thinking that after a few days I would go back to get it before another storm comes.

"Before I could go to bring the coal home, the wind started to blow again. I got ready and took a few sacks with me. I wanted to put the coal on top of the bank away from the sand. There it would be safe. As I went it got stormier and stormier. I said that to myself that I will be so tired if I have to take the coal up to the top of the bluff. That was too much for me. So I started to pray on my knees. I asked God to protect my coal, not to let the waves bother it. When I got through praying I went back home.

"The wind blew hard after I got home and I worried a bit. I thought that perhaps the coal would be gone. Then I said to myself, 'I have

Provision

prayed already. God has never failed me.' I said to myself in my little house."

The rest of the story became well known in Eskimo land. During the night the sou'wester increased in intensity, keeping everyone within the shelter of his own home for two days. When at last it subsided, a number of men hurriedly sledded out to check on the sacked coal they had placed on higher ground.

Acting in the kind of faith that doesn't panic, the older man followed with sacks he intended to fill for winter's use. In the meantime, those who had rushed ahead scanned their depleted reserves. Hungry waves had slashed into their piles, carrying away most of their coal that lay on supposedly secure ground.

Wait a minute. What's that over there? Onlookers stood speechless as others joined them to stand and stare. Well below the high water mark lay a heap of loose coal that the water hadn't touched.

To an outsider the presence of a few hundred pounds of coal may have appeared rather insignificant. Those who wrestled with nature for their livelihood, however, knew that the sea doesn't play favorites. Moving as if on hallowed ground, they got closer to the "sacred" mound. At last one of the

Alone in My Kayak

group with deep respect broke their stunned silence with, "That coal must be Patkotak's. He's a praying man."

No surprise to the owner. Didn't it happen in the Gospels that the waves obeyed Jesus? Patkotak's winter fuel made his neighbors do some serious thinking. They still joshed and bantered about his faith, but deep in their hearts they knew that strange things happened when he got down on his knees.

Then, like a surprise package, the Lord gave someone else the privilege of getting involved in an old man's needs. His son who lived nearby had gone out of town for a while when Patkotak, who stayed by himself, became ill. Getting down to the last bit of food in the house, he lay in bed wondering what to do. Would anyone think to check on him?

In simple faith Patkotak explained his need precisely as he saw it. "Lord, I don't know why I'm lying here sick when You are my Healer. But this I understand, that You want to teach me something through this. You see I have almost nothing to eat, but You are the God who fed Elijah as he sat alone by the brook.

"I'm hungry right now and wish I had some good hot cooked seal meat like my wife used to

Provision

like to cook for me. Please, God, You let someone cook seal meat in the village. Cause them to think to send some to me right away while I am praying.

"And, Lord," he added as if offering a practical suggestion to a friend, "If it's packed in cellophane paper it will hold nice and warm."

While he continued in praise and thanksgiving, a woman in another part of the village was cooking seal meat in a large pot. Suddenly she felt a strong impression that she must give some meat to Patkotak right away. Startled, the woman did as she felt she was being told.

Calling her son to come quickly, she thrust a package in his hand, sending him on an errand. "Hurry, and don't stop for anything. Run, quick!"

Before the man had finished his talk with God, he heard a knock at his door. In came a boy with steaming hot seal meat well wrapped in cellophane.

Chapter Thirteen

Balance

By design, a handmade *umiak* rides the waves lightly and is easily capsized if a man moves about recklessly. With careful stance, his feet centered on a caribou hide for sure footing, the whaling captain reaches for his weapon. Losing his balance means risking not only his own life, but also the lives of the entire crew.

Acquaintances feared that, figuratively speaking, Paul Patkotak might be "tipping the boat." He almost bent over backwards trying to do right, a tendency picked up from earlier associates. Starting on a basis of whatever wasn't spiritual was secular, they concluded that secular almost paralleled sinful. This mistaken view he had to overcome on his own while learning to discern the fine lines of right and wrong. He must be positive without becoming preachy, to hate sin without hating the sinner.

Neighbors knew the thick and thin of Patkotak and with each adjustment they saw more of Christ. As he matured, he also took what others said about him less seriously. Patkotak further learned that not all rules hold straight across the board either. He recalled when shooting a seal on Sunday was absolutely right; on another occasion, it might be totally wrong. How could he or anyone else be sure? There were no pat answers, for which reason the man chose to spend hours in the Word and in prayer.

Perhaps more than anything else, Patkotak set a premium on his hard-won freedom from fear. Determined to preserve it at any cost, he took a stand against Eskimo dances—a declaration readily mistaken for another "thou shalt not." Students of native culture describe two types of dances: stories or legends in pantomime and dances connected with demon worship. Patkotak couldn't be persuaded to take part in either. Although others saw no fault with the first, he wasn't making room for its combination of sight and sound to awaken

Balance

ugly specters of the past. What if that throbbing rhythm threw him back into the darkness he had escaped? Or planted within him desires contrary to his heartfelt convictions? He likewise felt a responsibility toward weaker Christians who might get carried away to excesses. It wasn't worth his taking that chance.

No doubt about it, Patkotak carried a "boring" label. A top hunter for sure, but he didn't do this and he didn't do that. Conscience also ruled him out of rap sessions that village men held under the shelter of upturned *umiaks* on the beach. He walked away from shady jokes and gossip. Neither would he take part in card games where solid family men lost their footing in gambling foils. Patkotak hurled the Bible quote, "Let him who thinks he stands take heed lest he fall" (I Cor. 10:12), with such fervor that listeners too often took it as an indictment. Those closest to him understood that the ominous warning applied as much to himself as to others. He was trying as best he knew how to keep his feet right in the center of the caribou skin.

What in the world did he do for recreation with no family at home and a social status that invoked little envy? When asked about his spare time, he smiled. His interests were so interwoven that Patkotak could hardly separate one from the other.

Fishing, beach combing, carving, reading, traveling with its unexpected excitements. "I like to cook too," he added. "I know how to take care of myself."

He was never hard up for something to do. Not the least, he liked to spend time worshiping God. Alone in his own house, he certainly wasn't praying to be heard. Occasionally his deep voice carried farther than he realized. If others overheard him, it didn't matter. No need to apologize for a heart overflowing with thanksgiving.

A little girl going out to play once tiptoed over to Patkotak's window. Having heard that he acted rather strangely at times, she wanted to see for herself. Sure enough. The old man was bowed in prayer, his face close to the floor.

"I came by again on my way home," Margaret told friends years later, "and peeked in his window again. There he was still praying. I was puzzled. I couldn't figure out what in the world a person could be praying about for so long."

"Did you laugh?"

"No, I didn't laugh. I didn't think anything. He was different from other people, but I didn't make fun. I wasn't afraid either because I understood he was like that."

Adults weren't always as tolerant of his peculiarities. Hadn't they also looked in on him as he knelt alone in prayer and again hours later as he paced the floor with hands upraised, praising God? Or speaking in a language no one else understood, clapping his hands for sheer joy? Come now, normal people just didn't do that. Few recognized the man's spontaneous outbursts for what they were. Unable to relate to his overwhelming emotions, they viewed him as someone who disrupted the accepted norm for their society. An unbiased panel, though, would have had to conclude that it was just as much his neighbors' reactions that caused the waves.

When pressures mounted, the village oddity walked out on the tundra or down to the beach for a breath of fresh air. There, drawing close to his heavenly Father, he found the comfort he needed. If he was upset, he simply stayed until he had "prayed through." With that he could return to face his world with a smile. He was perhaps a bit cautious, the label of "crazy" thwarting a spontaneous sparkle that might otherwise have asserted itself. Only Patkotak's family saw his unguarded personality.

"Our father often joked and teased," his children said. "He wasn't as serious as lots of people thought."

Once in a while he picked up the legends of his people. A favorite began with, "She was old like me, maybe older. The woman never had a gun, no weapon of any kind. She was just walking along, using her big stick to help her through the snow. She looked up. A polar bear was coming toward her."

The storyteller sprang to his feet, raising his arms and bending forward as if he were that feared king of the north. "Like this the bear came, standing up, ready to attack the woman. Quick she pulled off one of her big mittens. She stuck it on the end of her walking stick. When the bear came down with his mouth wide open, she could feel his breath.

"Like this," as he depicted further action, "that close. Then, then she rammed her big fur mitten right down his throat. The bear, he began choking, but he couldn't help himself. Rolling over in the snow. Choking. He forgot about the woman who ran back to the village fast as she could and called for hunters.

"When they got to the place, the bear was already dead. Choked to death. She had killed him with her mitten and her walking stick."

Patkotak's listeners who had heard the story dozens of times didn't register surprise. Neither

Balance

did anyone express disbelief, except perhaps for outsiders. Once a young man from another village muttered something about needing boots to wade through that kind of goop. His quick glance around the room for nods of approval at his clever remark met with stonefaced silence.

A Dane who had spent most of his life in isolated settlements along the coast of Greenland threw in his evaluation of the story with a positive, "Sure! I could believe that. I remember an old hunter with his left arm hanging useless at his side telling how, before the days of firearms, they went after polar bears single-handed. He described it like this: First the hunter finds the snow cave that he figures is a polar bear's home. He drops on all fours and creeps up to it slow-like to be sure it's not awake. He hopes his eyes will adjust quickly to the darkness inside, but if they don't it's still not the worst. He knows anyway how the bear sleeps, always curled up with his nose close to the air vent.

"With one arm up for defense, the killer crawls in. When the bear opens its mouth to attack, he thrusts his elbow as far as he can into those open jaws. He throws his weight to push its head up, exposing the throat. Then he plunges his knife deep into the bear's jugular vein. If he does it right, the fight is over in a minute.

"I can still see that old man telling his story, laughing about the way those big jaws clamped down." The Dane paused. "Laughing about his useless arm," he added as he shook his head incredulously. It went without saying that the hunter had chosen to risk his life in that way rather than starve to death. The laugh? Better to laugh than cry.

Reviving their legends kept the treasured past alive in the hearts of Patkotak's listeners. It also helped them to see that he was a real Inuit after all. Never mind some of his other quirks—you've got to respect a man who's got the guts to be different. Also, increased commerce proved that his earlier accounts of life Outside weren't as far-out as first thought either. In time a solid vote elected him to serve as president of the Wainwright village council.

Accepting the others' belated acceptance, Patkotak's reserve began to thaw. As he learned to relax more, he was able to evaluate incidents of years past and saw a two-way street.

"I had to learn to be patient with others just as God was patient with me," he said. "It took a long time for Him to teach me many things."

For about ten years he owned and operated a small store and curio shop. Between waiting on customers he carved ivory and made baskets of

Balance

baleen, the "strainers" from inside the whale's mouth. With a flare of imagination he made a tiny sled from the jaw bone of a fox and designed miniature ring holders from slices of whale tooth. His shop offered items not found in the usual tourist outlets.

He had to make a living, but Jesus was his real reason for living. With head bent over his work, he listened to those who came to him with their problems. "Promise you'll never tell, Patkotak?"

Nodding his head, the older man kept on with his work while a troubled neighbor poured out his hurts. Sometimes he only listened, other times he suggested a possible solution to a problem. Always he prayed, either then or in his quiet hours alone.

Closing the doors of home and shop, Patkotak unexpectedly announced his intentions of an extended trip into northern Canada. "What for, Dad?" his sons asked.

"Got to obey the Lord. That's what's most important, obeying the Lord."

That happened more than once, with Patkotak traveling at least part of the way during the summer by boat, in winter by dog team. Long hours of travel held their share of dangers and delays, but one could always find a corner by nightfall.

Whether he stayed a day or a week, native hospitality embraced him as one of the family.

On his first visit to Canada, he unwittingly followed the footprints of his brother, Richmond, who possessed an uncanny ability as a nature doctor. Often diagnosing illnesses with amazing accuracy, Richmond gave sound advice and even prescribed home remedies that brought relief. Though not a shaman, he wasn't averse to posing as one if it bettered his chances of helping someone. His success won the admiration of many of these distant relatives on his mother's side. Thinking that Patkotak might be endowed with like gifts, people flocked to him for similar treatment. No way, however, could he duplicate Richmond's talents.

He hastened to clarify his position. "I have no power to heal, but I know the God in Heaven and He is the greatest doctor to be found anywhere. You see that sun? Fire! God made that fire to keep you and me warm. God is good and He cares about us. He can heal your sick bodies and He can heal your sick souls."

Resentment mounted against this Alaskan with his simplistic talk about God. *What's he getting at? Trying to tell us we aren't good enough? Who does he think he is, anyway?*

Victory didn't come easy. Patkotak reviewed one of the darker episodes that took place far from home. "While I was there the old devil tried to hinder me. Even when I was sleeping he came right through the wall. You have never seen anything like it, so terrible and ugly. The devil looked like he never took a bath in his whole life!

"He said to me, 'I have come here to take away what you have in your heart. I don't want you to say a word about Jesus here.'

"But I answered straight back, 'You can never take away what I have in my heart. So you better get out *now* in Jesus' name!'

"You know what happened? He made a couple of turns and went through the wall, right where he came from."

Refusing the enemy some undue publicity, Patkotak referred to the above incident only when it seemed necessary to help believers comprehend spiritual warfare.

"I don't let myself think much about demons," he explained. "I would rather think about the Lord and feel good in my soul. We don't have to be curious about everything."

With that he changed the subject by concluding with a confident smile, "If God be for us, who can be against us?" (Rom. 8:31b)

In time people began to ask Patkotak for prayer and one after another recovered. Then he was asked to visit patients in the hospital, after which several were released. "What an encouragement," he reminisced, "seeing people stand up and realize they were well. To God be the glory! I feel like traveling on, no stopping along the way. Like a big ship out at sea—going along. Never stopping for storm, but just going right on."

Other opportunities for reaching the youth came when schoolteachers asked him to talk to their classes. He told about wanting an education, his travels, his struggles in face of obvious discrimination. Patkotak wished he could yank some of those students out of their chairs, make them jump up and see exciting things ahead. They had to believe in God and in His plan for their lives! So few of his people made an all-out effort to reach their potential. He, however, dared say it.

"Hey, I like that guy. He understands us. Maybe we ought to go see him. He talks our language." Teenagers gave positive responses to someone who had traveled their road.

"I would rather tell my story to the young ones," Patkotak conceded, "for they listen and believe." Those who knew him nodded their heads. The down-to-earthness of his faith appealed to the less sophisticated.

Balance

On subsequent trips, those who had once shunned him heralded his arrival. "The old man from Alaska is here again. The one who can pray to God and talk to us from the black Book is back."

Patkotak thrived on those evangelistic tours. A grandson described his return from one of his longer stays across the border. "I watched him get out of the plane, not like an old man. His feet were light, with spring in his steps. He moved quick and easy like a basketball player."

Back on the home front he picked up his old responsibilities. While traveling along the coast to set fox traps, Patkotak frequently stopped to gather driftwood. Carrying one's find to higher ground constituted valid claim. With no lumber yard within hundreds of miles, Patkotak carefully saved the better timbers for building sleds and meat racks. The rest he used for fuel. When he stopped for it on the way home, however, someone had already hustled it away. This happened time and again. He was sure he knew who was to blame, but he mentioned the loss to no one.

One day as Patkotak waited quietly in the presence of the Lord, he received an unmistakable order. "Go down river about 12 miles. There's a family in a tent and the husband is dying of tuberculosis."

Alone in My Kayak

Harnessing his dogs, Patkotak started down river immediately. When he stepped into the tent, the dying man gasped, "Oh, how I have wished that you would come! I'm going to die and I must confess that I stole your wood. Can you forgive me?"

"I knew well who the thief was," Patkotak replied kindly, "and I have already forgiven you. But you yourself have been stolen by another, a bigger thief, and only Jesus can save you from him."

"Then will you pray for me? You are so good at praying."

"It isn't a question of how good we can pray, but that we pray with a sincere heart. God is good and loves us all. He will free us from our sins because the sacrifice was paid at Calvary."

Patkotak led the young man to simple saving faith in God's Son and, like the thief on the cross, he reached out to accept the forgiveness so freely offered. The convert of a few hours slipped away with a smile of peace, his final whispers words of thanksgiving.

Joyfully the soul winner returned to his own home, praising God as he sledded along. To think that he had been divinely commissioned to carry

Balance

out an errand of eternal worth. How both humbled and honored can a person be?

After witnessing her husband's conversion, the wife of the dying man also accepted Jesus as her Savior. Her days too were numbered and a short time later she joined her husband on that other shore where there is no more sickness or pain.

Not long afterward another young fellow who lay dying called for Patkotak. "I'm sorry I made fun of you because you never smoke, you never dance. Forgive me," he begged.

The old disciple assured the one whose life was ebbing away that God loved him. "That man and the one who took my wood," he concluded reverently, "those were the two happiest dying men I have ever seen."

If anyone called him "preacher" either seriously or in fun, Patkotak shrugged it off. His early attempt when he first came back from Outside and his tours to Canada were the sum total of his public ministry. His call was to fill a need when he saw it, working most effectively on a one-to-one basis. He lived a full life. Heart-to-heart talks with Kayutak provided the safety valve he needed and community living had its rewards. One long stretch, though, appeared destined to pursue alone—commitment to prayer.

That doesn't mean no one else prayed, but, as the unknown author of the traditional spiritual penned, "You gotta walk that lonesome valley.... Nobody else can walk it for you. You gotta walk it by yourself."

Marking a path and smoothing out rough spots is never easy. When Patkotak was a long way around the bend, perhaps out of sight, others would pick up the trail and follow. Until then, God in His mercy would give high points enough to keep him "pressing on." The traveler, however, dared not use those peak experiences for campsites. When one sits too long enjoying his successes, that subtle enemy of the church—spiritual pride—will move in as quietly and deadly as pack ice.

As Patkotak often said, "...No stopping along the way. Like a big ship going along. Never stopping for storm, but just going right on."

Chapter Fourteen

Reinforcements

Patkotak threw a few things into his suitcase for another flight from Wainwright to the fast-growing township of Barrow. Naval installations, DEW line (Distant Early Warning radar sites) and private enterprises combined had whisked in changes. Rumors of possible oil findings near Prudhoe Bay followed. Older residents nodded their heads. They remembered picking up crusts of a tar-like substance that burned like blubber. Now geologists were saying that the black stuff had oozed up from underground oil deposits possibly centuries ago. Undoubtedly more of it lay in the earth's sealed vaults, waiting to be tapped.

An influx of workers brought new sights and sounds, even new sins—or at least new ways of committing the same old ones. In view of these, solid teachings of the church sounded too boring. The daring for flagrancy picked up speed like a runaway dog team, while efforts to address moral issues got laughed out the door. The total picture demanded nothing less than complete rejuvenation of the religious scene.

It had to start somewhere. Perhaps Sherman Duncklee, the Arctic Explorations employee who tried to have services at one of the movie *quonset* huts, held the key. Upon hearing about him, Patkotak made a quick trip to Barrow. The red-headed youth and Patkotak, whose dark hair was now streaked with silver, met and talked for hours. Recognizing that the church was no longer being reckoned with as a driving force in the community, they agreed on one point: The north would have to be jarred loose by an accelerated evangelistic thrust.

Patkotak returned to Wainwright in high spirits. He had at last found someone who saw the picture as he did. Figuratively speaking, someone had to rock the boat to get it moving out from the shore, but who and how? After all, another gospel outreach could be a touchy subject. Afraid of polarizing the Christian community, most folks

Reinforcements

would be quick to cast a negative vote if such were suggested. No one with an ounce of appreciation was about to play down the sacrificial efforts of stalwart pioneers like Stevenson and the Marshes. There were staunch contemporaries, supporters of the local church, whose exemplary lives demanded respect too. On the other hand, an unreached segment of the population deserved consideration—men like Ned who shrugged off godly admonitions as a joke, and women like Susan who stated matter-of-factly, "My family? We were just regular people who never went to church anywhere."

Patkotak and Sherman saw Barrow's problem as a double header: Not only did the established church need renewal, but further effort must be made to reach the unchurched. While Sherman expressed his desire to spearhead such a mission, he knew it would take someone with carpenter skills to lay the groundwork. Thus it came about that he referred the possibility of a new work to the Alvin and Lorraine Capener, Assembly of God missionaries in Nome. Someone else talked about "the top of the world" too: Thomas, a young man in jail who had turned a deaf ear to everyone who came there to minister. When he found himself "free" with nowhere to go, he ended up knocking at the Capeners' door. During his few days with them, Thomas talked incessantly about his home

Alone in My Kayak

town, Barrow. At last Capener decided to make a trip north to size up the situation for himself.

"When I visited the church already there," he later told friends, "I was pleased to see it nearly full. The 300 present was a fair number, but I saw ample room for another Christian witness in town of almost 2,000."

The Barrow to which new gospel workers came in 1954 boasted only a few streets with paths that wound round from one dwelling to another. A local fellow described it by telling an inquirer to scoop up a handful of gravel. "Now throw it," he ordered. "There you have it. Houses all over and any way. Maybe you walk all around a house to find the door."

How could one find property in such a place? Apparently squatter's rights were claim enough—if the newcomer didn't squat where there would some day be a street. Building supplies had to be ordered and shipped in on the once-a-year freighter, the *North Star*.

While waiting for their material, two of the workers began acquainting themselves with the town by knocking on doors. At a house next to the mission site they tried to make conversation with a young fellow who appeared totally uninterested in whatever they had to say. After a few awkward

Reinforcements

moments one of them asked, "Do you have a banjo?"

Momentarily stunned, the man stammered, "Yes. Uh, yes. I'll get it."

"How did he know I might have a banjo?" he puzzled to himself. Now guitars, everyone had those, but there weren't a lot of banjos around. Shades of his father, Paul Patkotak! They needn't explain why they were in town. He already knew.

Simeon went into another room to get his banjo. "Can you tune it?" as he handed it to the younger man.

After a few turns on the pegs, the mission worker strummed a cord and the men began to sing. As Patkotak's youngest son leaned back and listened, he was amazed even at himself. "I still can't believe it," he mused, "playing my banjo, singing about the Lord right here in my house. Well, they can't do any harm and the music is worth listening to, so I'll let it go."

When their building material arrived, the team began construction in freezing winds and plummeting temperatures. An occasional passerby stopped to offer a bit of timely advice or to lend a hand on the new meeting hall with temporary living quarters in the back. At the official opening,

Alone in My Kayak

which waited until after Christmas holidays, the people poured in. Among honest searchers and curiosity seekers sat Patkotak, who had come from Wainwright for the occasion. He had a feeling that this was what he had been waiting for.

That first week while Patkotak's son Steven was out hunting, his wife Jane attended every meeting at what was known as "the Assembly." They were respected citizens who worked hard and paid their bills. Yet all the while hunger for a personal relationship with the Lord Jesus Christ was growing in their hearts. When asked why she hesitated about making full commitment to the Lord, Jane paused before explaining, "I'm waiting for Steve. Then we can come together."

Upon Steven's return, they came to the meetings and together walked down the aisle to make public confession of their faith, the faith of his father.

Only weeks later Steven's brother Billy was flown in from Wainwright because of a back injury. With permission to leave the hospital, he walked over to the mission. At the first altar call he likewise went forward, confirming the dedication he had for some time intended to make.

"Hey, Patkotak, how do you feel about what's happening?" neighbors asked, indirectly extending congratulations.

"How do I feel? I feel good in my soul. Praise the Lord! Sometimes we wait long years, but just the same He is faithful. My God is real. Praise the Lord!"

Townsfolk smiled. If that old man could praise the Lord before, how much more now! Even if they themselves didn't choose to believe, well, it was good to see....

Chapter Fifteen

Revival

The scattered community of North Pole, south of Fairbanks, Alaska, offered challenge enough for Paul Bills to consider staying there indefinitely. He had no other plans until one day when, in reading his Bible, he picked up one brief command: "Set your house in order."

He paused. Was he being told he would die? He didn't think so—at least not right away.

"Hon," he approached his wife cautiously, "do you feel anything unusual, like maybe a change coming in our lives?"

Alone in My Kayak

"Change? No, I can't say that I feel anything."

Taking refuge in her assurance, the pastor ruled out the tragedy factor. Maybe, he speculated, they would be leaving North Pole. It seemed improbable, but....

No sooner had he shelved the thought than there came a letter asking them to fill in at the Barrow mission for a year. Perhaps, Capener suggested, they might even consider taking it on a permanent basis. The recipients tossed his proposal back and forth. Although not planning to relocate so soon, they had to admit to an earlier call to the Eskimo. Was this perhaps the time to move into that area?

Vexed by their own vacillating, the couple pleaded for divine guidance. Almost imperceptibly at first, a sure sense of direction took over: They must say good-bye to a church they had thought would be theirs for years to come.

They and their two adopted girls left Fairbanks in July with the mercury pushing toward 80 degrees. A few hours later the family set foot beyond the Arctic Circle in a biting wind of only a few notches above freezing. With Barrow not having an airport as such, incoming aircraft used the DEW Line landing strip. A covered truck with oversized tires met the incoming plane. Employees

Revival

hurriedly tossed suitcases, mail and an assortment of freight in the back. Last of all, passengers climbed in and hung on for dear life as they tried to get a narrow glimpse of Arctic scenery speeding past the open door.

Their "taxi" stopped at the church, an unimpressive building except perhaps for size. Even though a second story apartment had been added to the mission for adequate living quarters, the new tenants would soon learn it had a few quirks all its own. The furnace that consumed tons of coal belched soot and smoke at irregular intervals. For electricity they drew on the resources of two power companies and, if these failed, a 32-volt windmill. When the blades became so frost-laden that they could no longer turn, someone had to scrape off the accumulating ice. Pastor Bills climbed the tower—a daring maneuver that invariably took place when the winds blew their worst—while Marguerite watched from the window and prayed. Their water supply depended on the never-ending job of adding blocks of ice to a huge storage tank behind the furnace. Though using it sparingly, they counted water as one of their luxuries. "Plumbing out" was another story with no sewer lines laid in the permafrost, but a true missionary's physical comfort isn't first on the list anyway.

Alone in My Kayak

Already acquainted with summer and its outdoor pull, the Bills didn't feel let down with only 35 in the Sunday morning service. Evening attendance climbed to 75 and leveled. Campers coming home did little to boost the number, although in a few months the workers sensed a new "lift" in their worship services. But they were hardly making a dent in the community as a whole.

While the Bills discussed inviting an evangelist, a couple was already preparing to come—urbanites from a large church in southern California and the least likely of all candidates, except that no one else applied.

"After having visited Anchorage and surrounding towns," Oscar and Gladys Butterfield wrote, "we feel that the Lord would have us return north."

Pastor Bills paused. They didn't know what they were saying. No true Alaskan sees Anchorage as an introduction to the Arctic. Their letter did handle one matter convincingly, however: "With churches and friends backing us, we won't be a burden financially." That took care of the money, and references sounded reliable enough.

The couple arrived in mid-January with the weather living up to its reputation. The wind tried to push them back into the plane, but with heads lowered they made their way slowly down the icy steps. Oscar, a tall thin man in his late 50's, and Gladys, her husband's height with another hundred pounds, followed directions shouted by airport attendants. They climbed into the truck substituting as airport limousine and, with a spurt, were on their way.

A few minutes later the truck stopped. "This is it," the driver announced.

Peering through his window, a neighbor watched as Oscar and the driver worked to free Gladys from the back of the truck. He grinned. After watching them struggle with their baggage, however, his amusement faded into disgust. Turning to his drinking buddies, the onlooker vented his antipathy with a sneer. "Why would a church do that? Send in poor old white people who can't even jump on a truck or get in and out by themselves? They have to have help!"

Before the Bills realized that their guests had arrived, Oscar was making his way toward the main entrance. Gladys panted several paces behind him, the wind slapping her appropriately long gray dress, its hem wet from dragging in the snow piled on either side of the path. Oblivious to the scorn being directed their way, they beamed with happiness as they entered the mission.

Alone in My Kayak

Greeting the newcomers, the pastor secretly wondered what he had gotten himself into. Would his congregation, let alone outsiders, accept these city folks? Acceptance it had to be, or an empty meeting hall. If only he'd asked for their picture before giving his okay.... Could they handle the inconveniences, culture shock and all the rest? To his wife he later confided his doubts before adding one strong upbeat impression, "We have to say this for them, they look like they're ready for whatever comes."

Sunday morning's attendance edged up to about 75 people. During a rousing song service Gladys strummed a ukelele that looked more like a child's toy. Her gray-white hair that was pulled back into a tight bun let only a few short whisps slip free around a full face carrying a perpetual smile. An amused congregation smiling in return brought out the best in her. She beamed with happiness. When Oscar announced that his wife would sing, she stood to her feet and pulled at her dress that clung to her with static electricity. Tug here, yank there, and never hanging properly. Children snickered; adults waited patiently. At last Gladys began, her thin little-girl voice adding to the smiles. But the levity didn't last long, for the words of her song introduced the evening's message—and it was serious.

Revival

Oscar, a rapid-fire speaker who couldn't be bothered with an interpreter, came across in an authoritative manner that made the people sit up and listen. Never before had they been confronted by that kind of a sawdust-trail presentation.

"Did you hear...?" "Were you there?"

Word-of-mouth advertising shot the evening's attendance up to 150, stretching the sanctuary's capacity to the limit. The crowd was willing to sit three-deep if need be. A mother held her ten-year-old who in turn hugged a two-year-old tightly. Gaps between the benches were chinked with youngsters, not all of whom meant to sit through the preaching. Yet the general disturbance they created failed to dampen the fervor of the meeting.

Several responded to the invitation to make public their intention to live for Jesus. Tuesday night saw a packed house with more people threading their way down the aisle. Trying to step around those seated on the floor, they got snagged by wires of a dozen tape recorders—sure proof that when desperate for God, getting tripped enroute matters little. Wednesday night the lights went out. Someone brought in a gas lantern, pumping it vigorously to cast more light and shadows until the current came on again. Oscar preached on as if he were in the Orange Bowl's stadium under floodlights.

At the close of every service Patkotak, the gentle grandfather, knelt beside those who waveringly confessed their sin. Forgiveness they gladly accepted, but what if they couldn't hold out? With his well-worn Bible open, he pointed to a verse. "It says He will keep the feet of his saints," he quoted both in English and in Inupiaq.

"Claim God's promises," the veteran urged, knowing how he had held fast to an assurance the Lord gave him long ago for his family. His sons had been coming one by one. The youngest, with no intentions of being part of the church crowd, however, stayed away. He and his brother-in-law were getting ready for a caribou hunt. Revival? Prayer? Get off of it!

Disgruntled, Simeon stared glumly out the window. There was that preacher again—chipping off the yellow where stray dogs had availed themselves of ice blocks stacked up for winter water supply. After cleaning a block Brother Bills carried it indoors, dropping the chunk into their huge water tank to melt. Obviously not minding this daily chore, he came back out to work on another.

"That poor guy," the young man muttered angrily to himself. "One of the silliest fellows I

Revival

ever ran into. Why does he have to smile when he's cleaning up the ice?"

Simeon couldn't pinpoint what was eating him, only that he was soured on the world and everyone in it. Fanatics streamed past his house on their way to church as if to a movie or something. Count him out. What he didn't know was that the Holy Spirit had already counted him in.

"January 18, 1959," Simeon recalls. "I'll never forget that date. I really didn't get through in the morning, but in the evening I did. I was on my feet already—didn't know it until there I was facing the people. That was the greatest feeling I had in all my life, a clean feeling inside and out. Praise God, I got it! People had been talking about how the Lord can save a person. My father taught us, but when I got older I tried to get away from it. Only his prayers didn't go away.

"The next morning I felt so good when I went out. It was like whole Barrow was smiling at me. I can't describe it. The joy that can come into you is the real thing. I never used to look at people, especially preachers—Presbyterian or whoever. When I knew they were ministers of God, I went the other way. I was against them, but that was because of sin in my heart. This day it was different."

Early the following morning the older Patkotak went to his son's home to have devotions with Simeon and Susan.

Alone in My Kayak

"Feelings are wonderful," he emphasized, "but we have to get into the Word. It shows us how to live."

Patkotak made the rounds, visiting family and friends. He had always walked erect, his head up, but now his steps were quicker. His tears in secret had been rewarded openly. Observing the dramatic renewal of the man who had passed his sixty-seventh birthday, Pastor Bills sat down to his typewriter. The story wouldn't fall into place.

"Better wait," he told himself as he laid the paper aside, "until God calls Brother Paul home." Then I'll weave his story around the words of the old Simeon in the temple: 'Lord, now lettest Thou Thy servant depart in peace, according to Thy word: for mine eyes have seen Thy salvation'" (Luke 2:29-30). It was an unwritten story others would have reason to recall a few short years down the road.

Marguerite made her own observations at the height of revival. "I prayed for this, sure it would solve every difficult situation we or any of our congregation faced. Revival did take care of problems, but it also brought a whole lot more! More people, more problems. But don't get me wrong, for the Lord can take care of these problems!"

When a person comes to Christ he's like a little green apple—reckoned perfect in that he has no worm holes, no scab, no blight. He's clean through the blood of Jesus. But it takes hanging on through sunshine and rain for that apple to mature. The revival produced a basketful of green apples.

On the edge of the basket sat a get-rich-quick bunch who presumed that a spiritual touch meant they "got it all." Bypassing Christian growth, they would in time fall off. Neither did everyone praying the sinner's prayer follow through on his promissory note. The idea of sins forgiven had immediate appeal, but serious commitment?

By the time the evangelists left, various segments were also starting to go their own way. Then there was that nucleus—God love 'em—who got the full impact of Stuart Hamblen's song:

> It is no secret what God can do,
> What He's done for others, He'll do for you,
> With arms wide open, He'll pardon you,
> It is no secret what God can do.

The second stanza asks a question: "Someone slipped and fell, was that someone you?"

"Yes, Lord, it was me," the honest soul said as he dropped to his knees asking for cleansing. The old past had been taken care of, but the more recent past got smeared in an off-guarded moment. Those believers were given a promise: "If we confess our sins, He is faithful and just to forgive us our sins, and to cleanse us from all unrighteousness" (I John 1:9).

Alone in My Kayak

The uninitiated might have viewed these altar services with a mixture of merriment, puzzlement or even disdain. Dedicated workers described those same scenes as beautiful. While some knelt with bowed heads, others dared to lift tear-stained faces heavenward as they whispered, "Thank You."

A few feet away an overwrought teenager all but yelled, "Fill my need, Lord. Oh, Lord! Ohhh Lo-o-ord!"

Someone knelt beside him, placing an assuring arm round his shoulders. "God hears you and He wants to meet your need even more than you want Him to, so don't worry. Don't struggle. Just relax and talk to the Lord. He loves you and He's ready to listen."

Soothing tones quieted the frenzied youth who had somehow picked up the idea that he must call down fire from Heaven. In all fairness we have to understand the stranger who glanced around the room and breathed, "What in the world goes on here?" Once in a while the workers too had to smile.

Four of the new converts went out one night and stole a case of beer. Christians? Put it this way: They had lots to learn. Anyway, they got drunk and, for their good, were arrested. As soon as they were released, two of them showed up at the church office. Before the missionary could ask a question, they fell to their knees sobbing.

"Oh, Pastor," one of them blurted out. "The devil is getting stronger!"

So "Onward, Christian Soldiers" is more than a Sunday school song after all. War had been declared and each for himself would have to be adult enough to stand up and fight.

Smack in the middle of the revival a new conflict arose. Church loyalty, like true steel, needs tempering. While one group sang with fervor, "I'm going through, I'm going through," a group in another building was singing louder than they had in years, "I shall not be, I shall not be moved!"

Even if animosity had no place in their banter, it could invite danger. In the world of sports it's okay to cheer for the home team, but this mini-battle in the church could edge its way past being funny. It's the kind of story that gets blown up as a "real church fight." The non-churchgoers can use it to justify their staying away altogether. With conscience salved they go hunting on Sunday, assuring themselves that *they* (the spiritual ones) worship God in nature.

In their concern for the unconverted, Paul Bills and John Chambers of the Presbyterian church

Alone in My Kayak

met on common ground. John was a dedicated missionary who piloted his own plane to the outlying areas whenever he was needed. When a death occurred at a remote site, he was there within a few hours if weather permitted. The two clergymen engaged in serious talks aimed at eliminating factions and friction. Although not seeing eye-to-eye on all issues, they respected one another's positions. Each wanted to build his own congregation, but not at the cost of *who* would reach the lost. For a while it looked as if the fledgling work would far outstrip the established church, but final count showed otherwise. Enough Presbyterians got revived to more than fill the vacancies left by those who moved over to the Assembly, while both groups had the joy of nurturing new converts.

A less obvious danger threatened the workers themselves. No way could they duplicate the evangelists' efforts with services every night, but night owls who slept till noon wanted them. Days were already filled with people coming for help or to ask about Bible verses they didn't understand. Others popped in to see the latest goings on at the mission. Before the missionaries reached a breaking point, the situation resolved itself with believers meeting on their own. Looking back, those who attended shook their heads in wonder at the flow of their home meetings.

"How did we know where to meet?" One of them puzzled. "We never had a set place, but we had a feeling anyway of where to go. Before long we'd be gathered together in someone's house. We brought our tape recorders and later five-volt oscillators so we could reach all of Barrow.

"After we had prayer, we got on the air when one of the fellows announced the program, Showers of Blessing. We sent tapes along the coast, all the way over to Canada. This went on for months. That way we encouraged each other. Those who used to have problems like drinking and needed someplace to go to get away from temptation came every night. They grew in the Lord and got strong."

No longer singled out as "different," Patkotak lived it up, basking in the fellowship of other believers.

Lillian, a lovely Christian woman living there at the time, laughed, "I remember when he and my old dad who stayed Presbyterian came to eat. I set the food on the table half cooked. When the men sat down, they prayed for the food. They prayed for people and their needs, pray and pray. Maybe half an hour they prayed. When they got through, I told them I needed to warm up the food and put it back on the stove. That way it wasn't overcooked and everything was fine."

Patkotak had friends in both congregations, but chose to identify himself with the Assembly. Thus he had walked a full circle, coming back to being "Brother Paul" again. When a service was opened for testimonies, he always got his turn. "This is the Word of God," he called out. "It shows us the way to go. Hallelujah!"

His closing too was almost always the same. "When I get to Heaven, don't look for me just inside the eastern gate. I'll be at the *north* gate. Hallelujah!"

His church family, knowing pretty well what he was going to say, punctuated his sentences with amens anyway. Looking back on his years of consistent godly living when the going was rough, many of them felt a twinge of regret. If only they had shown him more compassion back then.

"Okay. If he was crazy then, we're all crazy with him now," someone commented as she watched him walking up and down the aisles with upraised hands and praising God.

"There he goes again," another chuckled, "the happiest man in the Arctic!"

"For years," Patkotak concluded in his own picturesque speech, "I paddled for the Lord alone in my kayak. Now we row many of us together in a big *umiak*. Praise the Lord! My God is real and He is so good!"

Chapter Sixteen

Ned Nusunginya

"Hey! Guess who just got saved? Ned!"

"Ned? You mean Nusunginya?" people asked.

"That's what I said. Ned!"

It couldn't be. He was the bad guy, or so ran his reputation. Standing alongside him made his neighbors feel at least better than the next person. When caught red-handed, or maybe when not even guilty at all, he would matter-of-factly take the blame. It wasn't Ned's habit to cop out with, "He (friend, relative or devil himself) made me do

Alone in My Kayak

it." Ned was Ned without excuses and without apology to anyone.

Opposites though they were, he and Patkotak were both ahead of their times. Aside from being Inuits who liked to hunt and who loved their families, whatever one was for, the other appeared to be against. Some folk called Ned plucky; others referred to him as scrappy. Either adjective fit the wiry fellow who accepted without complex his full height of five foot one. Strong-willed, set in his ways, he forged ahead to the point of being overassertive until one day.... But that character-changing episode was to come a long way down the road.

Ned, seven years younger than Patkotak, was born in Barrow in 1898. Although whalers from afar had already nudged against their shores, his growing-up years weren't much different from those of preceding generations, with one exception. He had the advantage of three or four scant years of schooling under early Presbyterian missionaries. This introduction to the printed page served as a springboard for devouring whatever he could get his hands on. By sheer determination he upgraded his education until his firm grip of the English language qualified him to serve as an interpreter. The church could use him,

Ned Nusunginya

but stay with it? He was too restless, too reckless, for that.

In 1917 Ned married Mimmealook, more often called by her English name, Faye. The one syllable fit this wisp of a girl a few inches shorter than her husband and, in her own quiet way, just as adventuresome. Ned set his mind to provide well for his bride. Though an outstanding hunter, he would rise above subsistence-living level.

In the early 20's when the mail route between Barrow and Kotzebue, a distance of about 400 miles one way, was opened, he applied. He knew that he and his team of 12 well-trained huskies could handle it. During a normal winter, November through April, he made three round trips averaging six weeks each. Occasionally his wife with their first child on her back under her parka rode along as far as Wainwright where she stayed with her parents until her husband's return. Faye recalls the winter she chose to remain in Barrow when he left in November for Unalakleet. Detained by uncooperative weather, Ned didn't make it back until February.

The carriers had one assignment: Get the mail through. They probably knew little about the workings of the postal system itself, nor had they heard the now-famous slogan chiseled into the stone facade of the General Post Office building in New York:

> Neither snow, nor rain, nor heat,
> nor gloom of night stays these
> couriers from the swift completion
> of their appointed rounds.

The architect, William Kendall, probably hadn't heard of anyone transporting mail across the frozen tundra either. For his part, Ned filled those classic lines to the letter, even to the "heat" when at the end of a long run he pulled off his sweaty inner parka. He mushed his team across wide-open country without trees or bushes for landmarks. There was no sun from mid-November until mid-January; no solid shelters for miles on end; no wood or fuel with which to build a fire. Howling winds, blinding snow and deep sub-zero temperatures simply served as incentives to keep him pushing on.

After one severe blizzard Ned reported losing his first five dogs—they had fallen dead in their tracks. Their lungs froze instantly as they gasped for breath while making a desperate lunge into the oncoming snow. The man made it through, pushing the sled himself to help make up for the loss of almost half his team.

"How could you stand it? How could you keep going?"

"The colder it is, the better I like it," the sledder replied without hesitation.

The mail run frequently accommodated passengers, one in particular whom Ned never forgot. Although Ronald Amundsen had received wide acclaim in the field of exploration, Ned wasn't impressed. With recognition enough among his own people, he needn't back down for anyone nor extend favors. "You ride. I'll handle the dogs," applied to one and all.

The noted Norwegian in his own profession had been in the driver's seat too. Navigating the Northwest Passage from the Atlantic to the Pacific, he helped pinpoint the location of the magnetic North Pole. Another ambition followed: to be the first to plant his country's flag where "going north" becomes "going south." Amundsen outfitted a ship and made other extensive preparations to reach his goal. Just before he started out, however, telegraph wires crackled the news that an American, Admiral Peary, had made it. Determined to cut his notch somewhere, Amundsen slipped out of Norway secretly. He meant to be the first to arrive at the South Pole even though he knew Robert Scott of Britain had already started out.

Amundsen receives credit for no small achievement; he and his dogs competed against a well-organized expedition that included ponies and motorized equipment. Scott and his men arrived at the South Pole a month later, only to lose their lives to cold and starvation on their return trip. The winner could have retired then with laurels if his heart wasn't still in the north. Perhaps he could make his mark by being the first to fly over the North Pole.

Outfitting a dirigible christened *Norge* in honor of his homeland, and making some swift moves, he arrived in Barrow ahead of schedule. His dirigible, however, developed last-minute mechanical problems. With luck seemingly against him, the explorer grew nervous and edgy. He had to get to the telegraph station in Nome immediately to order necessary parts. But how?

Hearing that Nusunginya was the best musher around, he hired him on the spot. Years later Ned credited the famous Scandinavian with being the toughest man he had ever met. Amundsen might have said the same for him. To save miles, they decided to cut across the ocean ice, which would have been easy enough had the wind not suddenly changed on them. Ned, who knew his own territory, realized the danger of being carried out to sea. They had better head toward shore and follow a longer overland route. Amundsen, with so much at stake, opposed Ned, egging him on against his better judgment.

Conditions worsened, and icy spray coated them like statues. Swallowing his pride, the near-frozen explorer finally begged Ned to stop, but by then the stubborn musher was out to prove he could hang in there. He'd give that Norwegian exactly what he asked for. "You wanted to go, so on we go," he yelled above the howling wind.

Upon arriving in Kotzebue, Ned had only one flat statement to make. "I'm through."

When his passenger implored him to complete the journey to Nome, the weary mail carrier refused to discuss terms or accept amends. "I've had enough," he replied. "Get someone else to take you."

Ned walked off the job, leaving a distraught Amundsen to scout around for other means of travel. He eventually made it back to Barrow and crossed over the pole—two days after the American explorers, Richard E. Byrd and Floyd Bennett, had won their fame in a small airplane.

At the news Ned only shrugged his shoulders. His first responsibility was the mail, not looking after passengers. Shortly afterwards he gave up the mail run. His reason? The postal department cut the route in half, with the first carrier going only as far as Point Hope. Ned couldn't tolerate

Alone in My Kayak

waiting for the relay team that was slower than he. He had hired out to get the mail through, not stand there and wait for it.

As for employment, if there was any to be had, he would find it. Between jobs in Barrow he made his living off land and sea until some years later when the DEW Line contractors needed a man to act as liaison with the villagers. Ned became hiring supervisor. As well as being bilingual, he could work with two thought patterns—that of the leader who wanted to get on with the job as well as of the native who'd rather skip a day to go hunting. An authority on Arctic conditions, his expertise proved invaluable to the development of the Arctic, a fact clearly established in 1955 when a period of unprecedented cold threatened the north coast.

The freighter, *North Star*, couldn't make it to Barrow. Under normal conditions, ocean ice lie reasonably far out until the latter part of August. That year it hugged the shore. After waiting several days without any appreciable change in weather, the ship's captain feared getting icebound. Seeing no way to move ahead, he considered returning to Seattle with the year's order of food, lumber and other supplies that Barrow residents counted on.

In desperation, several men in charge of construction chartered a small plane to fly over the scene in search of a possible open lead. Suddenly

Ned Nusunginya

one of them pointed to a lone figure with his dog team.

"See that fellow? Ned Nusunginya. He knows this country and he knows the ice better than any other man living. If we ask him what to do, he might be able to pull us out of this."

Unquestionably their man for the hour, Ned directed a crew out on the ice. "Here," he pointed.

Without further question, workmen planted dynamite and waited. When he judged climatic conditions and unseen forces beneath the ice as being just right, Ned ordered the blast. A path opened for the ship to proceed ahead for unloading. How did he figure it?

"Ned? That guy sniffs the current," his peers muttered.

Their amusing explanation brought a peal of laughter, but no comment from Ned.

What puzzled a lot of folks was why, without stooping to buy favors from anyone, he showed respect toward and helped gospel workers as much as he dared. As much as he dared? Well, he did have his own reputation to consider....

The early medical missionary, Dr. Greist, wanted Ned as his interpreter. His controversial spokesman had reasons, however, for feeling a bit uneasy when the minister touched on certain sins. Years later he confessed that he had embroidered Greist's sermons enough to make himself look at least passable. That couldn't go on for, in spite of other faults, underhandedness wasn't his game. He begged off, sure that he would never again interpret in church.

The man wasn't as hard as he let on. He cared for his family and took time with his children, whom he taught "Eskimo way" while also insisting on proper schooling. Faye took their ten children to Sunday school and church, a habit regarded by their father as commendable. For them, but not for him.

In 1952 the proud hunter reeled backward under a staggering blow—his son, Ned junior, lost his life in an accident. The grieving parents began making plans for the funeral. *Come now, what's this? Their son couldn't have proper burial because of his father's sins?*

Ned and Faye looked at each other in disbelief. It couldn't be! But the ruling stood. A committee with some degree of influence had seized upon this heartless means of disciplining their wayward neighbor. "That'll learn him a lesson," the wise ones clucked.

Ned Nusunginya

As for the Nusunginyas, the hurt went deep. Years later Ned confided how he had gone out on the tundra by himself to pray, "God, if there is a God, send us help. Send someone...."

People saw an unbending exterior, an embittered man who owned up to no lessons learned from the galling dose. If anything he went from bad to worse. God, however, looked deeper and saw a broken heart.

Faye, together with other family members, began attending the new mission. During meetings with Oscar and Gladys Butterfield, Ned went along. He sat quietly, obviously interested though careful not to appear emotionally involved. One afternoon Ned knocked at the Bills' door to offer a practical suggestion. The older people, he explained, couldn't follow English well enough to get the full benefit of the preaching. He would be glad to serve as interpreter.

Brother Butterfield, an inspirational preacher who might "lose his message" if he were distracted in any way, wasn't keen on using a go-between. His wife, however, perked up. It was her turn to speak Friday night. Inasmush as her sermon was to be mostly a reading of her own personal testimony, she would like having an interpreter.

Pastor Bills stood to one side trying to get the woman's attention. He meant to negate what was being arranged, but Gladys never noticed him shaking his head. Although he wasn't personally acquainted with Ned, and neither did he accept all the rumors floating about, the minister nevertheless wanted to keep the sacred desk above reproach.

God's timing, Ned's night. Gladys read her story. Proud, independent, a capable nurse and knowing it, the woman had pushed her way through life. When she said, "Back up!" folks backed up. When she wanted control, she got it. Things went her way, or else, until she met the Master and surrendered to His love. He removed the guilt and the anger that had dogged her steps as long as she could remember.

Ned knew what she was talking about. After interpreting the message exactly as it was given, he stepped down from the platform to kneel with those coming forward. Jesus Christ came to save sinners—he qualified there. Would he be accepted? On the merits of God's grace, yes. The self-made man crumbled, weeping his way to Calvary. His prayer out on the tundra was being answered by a God who loved him enough to forgive and to extend a clean slate.

Ned had filled his threescore years, but life for him had just begun. Investing in a recorder, he sent messages everywhere to announce that he was now a new man. After that he hitched up his dogs and once more followed his mail route of bygone days. This time he carried personally the news that the old Nusunginya was dead. He was a new man, born of the Spirit—and now he and Paul Patkotak were brothers in Christ. Folk wouldn't have believed it if they hadn't seen it, these two unique personalities lifting their voices together in praise to God.

Trying to make up for lost years, Ned met with his pastor every morning for Bible study and prayer. Besides filling the role of interpreter, he became teacher of the adult Bible class. One morning this older student opened his heart to Pastor Bills. "God is calling me," he stated with firm conviction. "I like working here with you, but I must go out and minister to my people."

Ned's preparation for the ministry had already been going on under Pastor Bills. He then took Far North Bible School classes under Dr. Arvin Glandon and later enrolled in Berean Bible Correspondence courses. His perseverance merited the waiving of some lesser educational requirements. Shortly thereafter his daughter Mabel took over his Bible class as he and Faye moved 300 miles east

Alone in My Kayak

to Kaktovik to pastor the mission there. It was after his seventieth birthday that Ned became the first Eskimo ordained to the ministry by his denomination, and perhaps the oldest person to receive this initial honor.

Serving the Lord didn't lessen his reputation as a hunter, however. "Him?" his neighbors offered in serious humor. "That guy can even think like a whale!"

When snowmobiles became available, he chose the "iron dog" over his ever-hungry huskies. Once when out hunting some distance from Kaktovik, Ned herded a polar bear into the village, cowboy style, and shot it there. The account made interesting reading in Fairbanks newspapers, but Ned didn't see his escapade as anything to write about. Common sense should tell anyone that there's no need to kill and transport meat when a living bear is well able to carry its own weight.

Another time when returning to their camp he spotted a wolverine. His gun jammed, but Ned wasn't to be outwitted. Like an old ranch hand rounding up a stray, he rode to the right and to the left in close pursuit of the near-frantic animal. Back at camp Faye heard the fast and slow, high and low of the motor as he swerved first from one side. She knew her husband was chasing something, but she didn't get the message soon enough.

Ned Nusunginya

The fleeing wolverine ran right through camp on his way to pant to the other wolverines, "You won't believe this one!"

Faye more than made up for missing it. Almost every September after the children were grown, the call of the wild got to her. Ned understood. Loading a sled with supplies, he took her to a camp where she stayed until mid-October.

"I like hooking," she explained.

"Then you got lots of fish?"

"Not really," she chuckled, covering her mouth with her hand in a half-embarrassed gesture, "because I get caribou too. Sometimes my husband chartered a small plane to come out and see how I was getting along. When I was ready to go home, he come with his team to get me."

Ned pastored well, making improvements on the church building, blending into the community. The area in which he felt his deepest sense of accomplishment, however, was teaching the Word that he had learned to love. After four years the couple moved to Point Hope, a larger village where he preached to a sizeable congregation. They were enjoying *nulakatuq* (whale days) in the spring of 1972 when Ned suffered a slight heart attack. He was flown out immediately for medical attention, but in less than a month his body was flown back to the far north. There it awaits that trumpet sound when our bodies rise to join our spirits—ever to be with the Lord.

Paul Patkotak lived on. In quiet moments he might have wondered why this younger brother who had moved up in the ranks to become a pastor and teacher was taken before he was. Ned's light had shone brightly, but briefly. Patkotak's didn't seem quite as bright, but it had shone steadily over several decades.

Which is the greater? That's not ours to say, for earthly classifications don't tell the whole story. Each must walk the path laid out for him. For Patkotak it might mean more trail to break, clearing the way for others yet to follow.

Chapter Seventeen

Wainwright

Several months after the breakthrough in Barrow, "the happiest man in the Arctic" went back to Wainwright. Reports of the meetings had gone ahead of him. People discussed the changes that had come over many of their acquaintances who had embraced Patkotak's religion. Turned over a new leaf, sure. But how long would it last? It was worth a wager, maybe.

The older man had won their respect, but they didn't owe him a following. Neither were some of the more levelheaded ones going to get swept away by a religious fad. For them the better part of

Alone in My Kayak

good judgment said to take it slow.... The slow part of it seemed slower than ever to Patkotak. Why couldn't they see revival right there in his home town? Maybe it would speed things up if he made a trip to Barrow to remind Pastor Bills of their need.

Patkotak put feet to his prayers, literally, when he decided to make the journey on foot. Having dogteamed that 80-mile stretch in his younger days, he knew of shelters along the way. He had the money for a plane ticket, but he craved hours alone to pray without distraction.

"Come in," the missionary responded to a soft rap on his study door. Patkotak stepped into the room, his fur parka radiating cold, the ruff close to his face hanging heavy with frost. His steps seemed a fraction slower than usual as he walked across the room and dropped his weight into a chair. Bypassing customary greetings, yet without laying aside his characteristic dignity, the man leaned toward the minister.

"Brother Bills," he pleaded hoarsely, "Don't you know of somebody who can come to my village to help our people understand the gospel?"

The pastor was at that very moment holding a letter from a woman ministering in a fishing town in northern Maine.

Wainwright

"God has given me a vision of Eskimo people," she wrote. "Isn't there a place, perhaps a needy village near you, that hasn't yet received the full gospel message?"

The timing of Patkotak's brief visit just as he was reading her letter compelled Pastor Bills to reply positively, suggesting that she come to Alaska at once. Obviously, Patkotak's urge to present the need of Wainwright this one more time wasn't lack of faith. It furthered correspondence that might otherwise have been laid aside.

After visiting a few days with his children in Barrow, Patkotak returned to Wainwright where, one by one, he tore pages from his calendar. Why didn't he hear more from or about the person who had expressed an interest in coming? What he didn't know was that Cecilia Piper down on the coast of Maine had ripped open the letter postmarked Barrow to read an accurate description of the village she had seen in the Spirit. It was the verification she needed! At once she began winding up her work, as she would have to raise support for this new endeavor. If Patkotak was feeling the drag of time, he wasn't the only one. Almost two years went by before the prospective missionary could fly north.

During that interim the Capeners had returned to fill in at Barrow while the Bills family went out

Alone in My Kayak

on a year's furlough. After some months Patkotak decided to visit there again, and, as was his custom, went to church early. While waiting for the meeting to start, he glanced up just in time to see a tall woman with slightly graying hair come in. He looked more closely, studying a face he thought he recognized. Wait a minute—could it be?

Hardly able to contain his emotions, Patkotak rushed to the platform to share his elation with the missionary.

"I know that woman," he choked as he tugged at the leader's sleeve. "I saw her in a vision, standing on the shore at Wainwright when the *North Star* came in. She was receiving lumber as it was being unloaded for a new building. That's the woman. I know her."

Capener, a carpenter who knew precisely how he wanted things done, hesitated. He couldn't delay the song service to talk. The lady preacher would be staying with them a month before moving to Wainwright, but if there was to be any construction going on, he'd see it through from start to finish.

Cecilia went to Wainwright in December, 1959, holding meetings in the coffee shop and in private homes for almost a year. In the meantime Roy Ahmaogak, pastor of the Presbyterian church, and

Don Webster, who worked with the Wycliffe Bible Translators, viewed the opening of a new mission with honest misgivings. Although they stopped by once in a while to see her, they dared not let anything distract them from their assignment of translating the New Testament into Inupiaq. The task was already decades overdue. Occasionally, after laying aside their stacks of papers to relax with a cup of tea, disconcerting thoughts surfaced. What if their village of less than 50 homes became divided? Wouldn't it have been far better if this energetic woman had gone somewhere else? Webster especially felt put on the spot. In keeping with the policy of the society he represented, he must not discriminate between groups. That meant sooner or later he would be expected to cooperate with the incoming mission as well as to continue helping at the Presbyterian church.

A year later the village council approved the construction of a second church building within their bounds. Spring rolled into summer, clearing out the ice for the *North Star* to make its annual run. The freighter stayed only long enough for freight to be brought to shore as there was no wharf to receive the barrels, boxes and bundles consigned to the village. The storekeeper hired a crew to help with orders while teachers got students to assist them with school supplies. Almost everyone made it down to the beach—if not to get something, at least to savor the delightful commotion. For some reason the Barrow men who were to come and help with the new mission's supplies couldn't make it. Someone had to see that the goods were moved to location. So, there, amid all the coming and going, stood Cecilia Piper—no surprise to Patkotak, who had known all along exactly how it would be.

When the builders finally got to Wainwright, the lumber was there on site. They quickly went to work, erecting a meeting hall with living quarters before fall storms began. Cecilia moved into her new home in time to welcome her first guests, Oscar and Gladys Butterfield, who were making their second round of Alaskan villages. They arrived on the same plane that took Roy Ahmaogak out for a week. Solid church members wondered what would happen. Cat's away, the mice play, and especially in remote villages offering little else to break the monotony of everyday living.

The people packed out the new building, clapping their hands in accompaniment to the lively music. What followed could hardly be called entertainment designed to give folk the feel-betters. "God is a righteous God who cannot look on sin," the evangelist fired. "He sent His son Jesus who became sin for us. That means He took our place, and our sin was nailed to the cross of Calvary. But it's up to you and me to decide if we want to accept the salvation He offers."

Young people flocked to the front of the hall, kneeling at the altar and nearby benches. Tears of thankfulness to God, who specializes in the impossible, welled up within, spilling over first in repentance and then in worship. The Wycliffe translator waited until the second evening to attend the revival meeting. Not being accustomed to the informality of the services, he felt a bit skeptical. But, God helping him, he would be open and honest no matter what. There had to be something to the goings-on, for some of those tough customers up front wouldn't put on a religious act under threat of a firing squad!

"Help me, Lord."Webster prayed. "Help me to view this without prejudice."

No doubt what he witnessed was a sovereign move of God. He and his wife, who had already written letters home requesting prayer concerning the spiritual apathy of their coastal community, rejoiced at seeing the story reversed. Nonetheless, without jealousy or resentment, a certain undefinable ache filled their hearts. Why couldn't the same spiritual renewal take place under their ministry? How could God, who is not a

Alone in My Kayak

respecter of persons, bypass the Presbyterian body altogether? If they were open to the moving of the Holy Spirit, couldn't they also receive His promised blessing?

The following Sunday evening, Don, who was filling the pulpit during Roy's absence, walked slowly over to the church he had grown to love so dearly. With all the fervor and mounting enthusiasm of the Pentecostal revival going on a few doors away, would anyone come to their usual meeting place? Well before meeting time he saw people going the other direction. So be it. He would wait and pray, and minister to whoever came, even if it was only one.

To his surprise, steadfast members took their accustomed places, followed by others who hadn't been that faithful, until every seat was filled. In simplest terms the Wycliffe translator spoke from his heart through his interpreter Peter Tagarook.

"Revival occurs among God's people when they begin to take seriously what God has told them in His Word. To be filled with the Spirit means we depend upon God's Holy Spirit to lead and direct us in all the ordinary things we do in life. If we hunt or fish or teach school or visit the sick or work in a store, it is what He has chosen for us to do. We ask Him to lead us and direct us in our everyday life...."

Wainwright

Closing the service, Webster sat down, resting his face in his hands as he prayed silently. He heard chairs being pushed out of the way, scraping on the bare floor, one banging against another. Then he heard the shuffling of restless feet. His mind's eye saw the congregation filing out without receiving his usual handclasp at the door, but he didn't have what it took to get up. He had to pray. Later he'd apologize for what had sounded to him like a weak attempt at a sermon. Still, he had done his best and the Lord knew that too.

Gradually it occurred to the troubled minister that the outer door never opened. Instead, footsteps moved toward the front. What was going on? He glanced up. Without coaxing or invitation, the choir as a unit had left the platform. At the same instant young people who had been hanging on to his words started forward, everyone finding a place to pray. Elders and leaders followed. The entire congregation of about 70 (with the exception of three who remained seated) wept as they confessed their sin.

Men and women who had thought themselves already good enough were asking to be made clean, that they might serve God with a pure heart. Their leader could hardly believe what he was hearing. Surely God had answered his heart's cry! Sensitive to the Spirit's direction, he remained quiet. The Lord who instituted this move would see it through to completion. After 15 or 20 minutes various members stood up to testify, openly expressing the joy of burdens lifted. Others told of their unrest being replaced by indescribable peace. More than one sought out a former enemy to bring about reconciliation. Jubilation!

What would their pastor think of this unprecedented wave of revival taking place during his absence? Returning on Monday, he had hardly reached his house before a delegation of loyal elders came. Without so much as waiting for him to take off his parka, they began telling him what had taken place the previous evening. Great man that he was, Ahmaogak listened without lifting an eyebrow to express personal opinion or to pass judgment.

"I agree we should not polarize our community," he began wisely. "Also, it seems that I have indeed returned to a village different from what I left. What has happened is outside my experience, but I'll wait and see how God will use this new thing."

Because of the Ahmaogaks' and the Websters' open attitude, Wainwright, probably more than any other northern village, experienced a baptism of love. At the same time it was spared the awkward (in some instances near-fatal) period of adjustment that can follow such tremendous change. Their caring leadership helped thwart suspicions and fears. Petty jealousies wilted when touched by the fire of the Holy Spirit. Indifference changed to Hallelujahs! rebounding from church to church and echoing in between. Prayer meetings replaced card games; Bible studies moved out shallow rap sessions; friendliness erased long-standing feuds.

Polarization? Not even a spirit of competition tantalized the believers. Assembly leaders knew well that, but for a solid foundation laid by their predecessors, they wouldn't be where they are today. Likewise, Presbyterians realized that if someone hadn't jarred them out of their complacency, they would have dwindled to absolute powerlessness. They needed each other.

A question arose among a number of Assembly workers in Alaska: Rather than duplicate efforts, should they close their missions in villages where an established church was proclaiming the gospel in its entirety? They could simply back out and leave the field to the first comers. After weighing the issue carefully, however, it was generally agreed that withdrawal could create further misunderstanding. The established church might even be blamed for booting them out! A critical world needs to see unity of purpose in spite of less important differences.

People have a right to a choice. Churches, like individuals, reveal personalities. One smiles his greeting; another says "Hi!" and slaps a friend on the back. One enjoys hymns; another prefers singing choruses. Although our hearts be alike, our responses vary.

Problems deeper than personality, however, began to crop up in the village. An excited convert interpreted his dream (maybe brought on by too much seal meat) as a message from God. A minority carried away with a carnal concept of God's love thought it all right to get drunk occasionally as long as they came back to ask forgiveness. Others in their singing and praising the Lord forgot the balance that comes with the Word and prayer. The two pastors along with the Wycliffe couple were kept busy guiding new believers along safe paths.

As for Patkotak, seeing the churches grow both spiritually and numerically was enough to send him into orbit. Yet never was he heard taking credit for the revival. He knew what the Bible said about "prayers, intercessions, and giving of thanks... that we may lead a quiet and peaceable life in all godliness and honesty" (I Tim. 2:1-2).

Tranquil fulfillment. What else could he hope for, other than to be still needed?

One season blended into another. Then one day the *North Star* stopped by on its annual run servicing the villages. Unloading the ship again became the first order of business. The usual disarray of loose freight and odd-sized containers laid around waiting to be claimed. Not feeling like his usual spry self, Patkotak let others do the work while he watched the bustling activity from his window.

A man helping transport the heavier goods to the village proper admired a brand new vehicle being unloaded for Billy Patkotak. He backed his tractor up to the vehicle that was bolted immoveable for shipping and hooked on with a few links of tow chain, leaving a only a short space between. Climbing onto the tractor again, he inched ahead carefully to get moving without snapping the chain. Like a cumbersome toboggan, the load crept slowly over the rough terrain, the driver staring straight ahead to avoid unnecessary bumps.

Several children ran playfully alongside. They could keep up with this slowpoke! Steven, six or seven years old and a head taller than his playmates, jumped at a chance for a free ride. Missing both the tractor and its load, he got sandwiched in between. The roar of the motor drowned out his cries. His younger admirers, taking his frantic gestures as part of the game, laughed back at him.

The vehicle dragged the child about 150 yards, each jolt wedging him tighter. As they neared Billy Patkotak's home, Amy came out to see the vehicle they had ordered months before. She stood in shock—frozen as her gaze swept past the frolicking children and zeroed in on Steven. Others who saw it yelled at the driver, but he couldn't decipher their frenzied shouts.

In an instant Patkotak darted in front of the tractor, motioning for it to stop. Switching the key off and looking back, the man sickened with horror at the sight of the little stowaway. Patkotak ran back and tried to pry the boy loose. No give. Someone else bellied under the machine, but the child's dangling legs hindered the would-be rescuer from getting his hands in to unhook the chain. In a desperate effort to free the boy, other strong men came to hold on to the bulky load while the driver eased his tractor forward. At last they succeeded in relieving the pressure enough for Patkotak to grip Steven's shoulders and lift from the cruel vise what appeared to be a lifeless body.

Patkotak tenderly carried the limp form over to the knoll where he sat down. Not his grandchild, but someone's. Holding the boy on his lap and but someone's. Holding the boy on his lap and close to his heart he prayed to his God who had proven faithful time and again over a span of several decades. Suddenly the youngster's breath returned and he began to cry for his mommy and daddy.

Steven later told his parents that he had seen Jesus coming for him, but when he heard someone praying he came back to earth again. Inasmuch as planes serviced Wainwright only twice a week, the boy couldn't be flown in for an immediate check-up. Although he appeared unhurt, his parents nevertheless took him on the next available flight to the Barrow hospital.

"What do you find, Doctor?"

"Nothing. Not a trace of injury."

The village sang it, they shouted it—and they'll never forget it. "To God be the glory, great things He has done!"

Chapter Eighteen

Endurance

Patkotak's hair had turned snow white, but below thick, bushy brows his eyes shown clear and keen. He walked erect, though not with his usual quick steps. Neither was he taking long hikes across the rough terrain. Otherwise he felt good, for which he was thankful. No small wonder that his zest for life took a disheartening blow when a routine check-up revealed tuberculosis. Where was his all-sufficient God now?

"I was all alone in my house in Barrow. It was four o'clock in the morning," he told friends, "when the blood started to come through my mouth.

Alone in My Kayak

When I saw it coming, I felt discouraged. What's going to happen to me? While I was thinking troubled thoughts, I remembered what it says in the Bible, 'I am the Lord that healeth thee.'

"Holding a cloth over my mouth, I got up. It was early in the morning and I went to see the Assembly preacher. I woke him up and said, 'Brother Bills, I'm spitting blood. I want you to pray for me.'

"He put his hands on me and started to pray. I prayed too, calling on God to help me and to stop the hemorrhage. I felt better.

"I said, 'Let's go to my oldest son Steven and let him know what happened to me.'

"We knocked at the door and woke him up. He came and opened the door and saw me. "He said, 'What is it, Dad?'

"I said, 'Sonny, the blood comes out through my mouth.'

"And he said, 'Dad, don't worry. We'll call on God to help you and to stop the blood.'

"He started to pray for me and I didn't spit any more blood. I took deep breaths and no more pain. My son went back to bed. Then Brother Bills said to me, 'You go to see the doctor.'

Endurance

"I said, 'I don't need to go to the doctor. I'm healed.'

" 'I know it,' Brother Bills said. 'That's just why you should go and report. If you are healed, you have nothing to be afraid of.'

"I went over to the hospital. The doctor knew me and he had been waiting for me to die. He put me on a table, made me lie down under a big instrument, with a big glass like a great big looking glass. It took a long time and Brother Bills gave up waiting for me as he had things to do at home.

"When they were x-raying my lungs I had my mind on the Lord, saying in my heart, 'Lord, don't let them find anything in my lungs. I don't want to go to the hospital in Anchorage.'

"They used about two or three x-ray plates and the doctor and the head nurse went off to the side and whispered to themselves as they looked at the x-rays. After about half an hour the doctor came to me, close to my face and said, 'Paul, I think you better go home. There is no one in town healthier than you are. Your lungs are clear as can be.'

"You know, I felt like I wanted to cry and praise God. I went home, three or four blocks to where I stayed, praising God for answered prayer. He has been so good to me."

Alone in My Kayak

With strength renewed, Patkotak went to Canada again by plane. Never mind that he arrived unannounced. The mention of his name brought people together in homes, schools, community halls and churches. Once while speaking to an Eskimo congregation, he paused intermittently for the benefit of two Canadians and an American present. In a few brief sentences in English he would give them a condensed version of what he had just said.

After the meeting he apologized to the visitors. "I get to thinking about what I have to say and I forget those of you who don't understand our language. I'm sorry I never stop often and say as much as I should."

The three glanced at each other knowingly before one of them set him at ease with, "Don't worry about us. You needn't have interpreted more, for we understood."

They couldn't explain how, but they were able to follow his message as if he were speaking their language. The few explanations he had remembered to give only served to confirm that they were "hearing" correctly.

Whenever possible, Patkotak stopped enroute at Kaktovik, Barter Island, to visit some of Ethel's family. One day as he was standing near the post

Endurance

office, he noticed one of the local fellows talking to a newcomer. Gently nudging the local man aside with, "Let me tell my white brother what God has done for me," he reached out his hand to the stranger.

"My name is Paul Patkotak," he said, "and I want to tell you what God has done for me."

The man appeared stunned. Without a word he reached in his pocket and pulled out a worn piece of paper. Patkotak looked at it in surprise—a tract he had written years ago. "In my search for God," Charlie Evans explained later, "I had picked up a couple of tracts. One was Paul Patkotak's testimony of salvation and of an unusual experience he had as a young man. At a campmeeting he heard a message given in tongues, in his language, telling him that he was to return to his own people. The Lord had revealed His love to him so he in turn could show that love to other Eskimos who had a knowledge of God without really knowing Him in person.

"After I read it, I drove out to a wooded area alone and prayed, 'If you're real, God, and these aren't just made-up stories to get followers, then let me meet someone directly involved in one of these happenings.'"

A few months later Charlie was hired by the weather bureau, a job change that moved him

Alone in My Kayak

from Idaho to Alaska. After a short stint on the Aleutians, Charlie accepted a transfer of a couple thousand miles to the north slope.

"I'll always remember," he added with tears, "that the Lord let me meet the one person in all the world who could erase my doubts. There I was, shaking hands with Paul Patkotak—the man of God who was an answer to my prayer."

It was another one of the compensations that the Lord had stored up for Paul against his slowing-down days. Although realizing that his Canadian visits would soon be a thing of the past, he could face inevitable change with candor. The consecration of his youth had carried a commitment to do whatever God asked of him, even if "doing" meant sitting still. The words of a beloved hymn, by C. Austin Miles held no less meaning in forced retirement than back when he first learned to sing.

> But if to go or stay,
> Or whether here or there,
> I'll be with my Savior
> Content anywhere.

He remembered how as a young man he had prayed, "If you ask me to walk alone, Lord...." But God gave him Ethel and for 20 brief years they journeyed hand in hand. Then she was gone....

"If I have to give up hunting and fishing, Lord...." But God chose to prosper his living off the land. Now, buckling under frailties brought on by advancing age, he had to let go of the pleasure as well. Lay it on the line: "content anywhere."

He had seen a lot in his day, going back to the previous century. The first missionaries, Stevenson, the Marshes...the turn of the century...his teacher, Mrs. Spriggs...early pioneers who declared God's Word...people who listened.... It had been like the tide coming in with rich gifts from the ocean's floor.

After a while it began to appear as if the beaches were bare again, that people were hearing without hearing anymore. Maybe it was because they were so sure that they were all right. Then like another flood tide...another mission...unprecedented awakening...revival...his prayers over the years finally answered. Those were the days!

There was Paul Bills too, the man who meant to write Patkotak's story. He was on staff at Anchorage First Assembly when the doctor said, "You'd better set your house in order." The diagnosis: Amyotraphic Lateral Schlerosis (Lou Gehrig's disease). A year later he slipped away in his sleep. In keeping with his wishes, his wife had his body flown to Barrow on August 7, 1977 (his sixty-seventh birthday).

"Up there, where it's so cold...?"

"It was Paul's request," she replied, "that he be laid to rest by Ned, his Eskimo brother."

For Patkotak, yet another younger than he had crossed over to the other side, but that did not trouble him. History repeating itself with the spiritual flow declining, however, was hard to take. Patkotak could name people who came to Christ, but who turned back when the going got rough. Others, perhaps without meaning to, drifted away. The tide was going out—so far out that it looked like a return to shamanism with drugs and alcohol sending its devotees on weird trips. The old man especially hurt for the young people coming up. Few of their elders were able to encourage integrity from firsthand experience in their own youth. Patkotak couldn't help but think about Israel: "and there arose another generation...which knew not the Lord..." (Judg. 2:10b). It wasn't his place to condemn, but neither did he know how to change the events taking place around him. What could he do? Keep on praying, that's what. The spiritual renewal, wonderful as it was, faced the danger of being left to die on a sun-baked plateau. His people must understand that they had barely touched a lesser mountain peak. Beyond it lay another valley before a still higher ascent.

Endurance

"Lord, I'm afraid they might forget..."

Did he hear himself saying that they, other people, might forget? Who of us escapes that temptation? He too must stand guard lest, no longer having to battle alone, he relax his vigil. His own words came in reply: "No stopping along the way. Like a big ship out at sea—going along. Never stopping for storm, but just going right on."

Apparent setbacks notwithstanding, the north coast would never be the same again. Because of a divine visitation that in one way or another affected every home of the Brooks Range, the Church that has withstood the ravages of time was being added to. It was Jesus Himself who made that powerful declaration, "I will build My church; and the gates of hell shall not prevail against it" (Matt. 16:18).

The Church universal. Even though he reserved a natural soft spot for his own people, Patkotak continued to hurdle racial barriers. Purposely forgetting injustices that could have made him back off, he chose to remember an old debt. "I thank God," he said with deep feeling, "for the white people who came to us with the gospel."

Observing vacationers with time on their hands that wasn't always handled wisely, Patkotak's eyes filled with tears. "Those poor tourists need God!

Alone in My Kayak

They need to know about salvation, to know Jesus."

That yearning to touch people from every walk of life provided another outreach. Sitting by his window, he waited for the summer tour bus bringing sightseers in from the airport. The guide, hard pressed for attractive sites along his short route, included the three churches among points of special interest for his passengers. The *quonset*-type Catholic church hedged in between larger structures was seldom open unless a visiting priest came to town. The Presbyterian church built in 1910 (the original building was destroyed by fire in 1909) rated highest in historical value. By the time the tour reached the Assembly's boxlike meeting hall, Patkotak was already inside and waiting. Before opening the double doors though, the guide lifted the lid of the ice cellar near its main entrance. Tourists excitedly snapped pictures of the deep freeze, a sizeable well with a long ladder extending downward into the darkness. Maybe their flashbulbs would pick up more than what their eyes could see.

Then they entered the sanctuary itself. Respectfully searching for something worth photographing, they filed in. Taking the guide's brief, "Here it is," as his cue, an older man stood to his feet. In a heavy but well-enunciated accent he began his

Endurance

life's story, recounting the hungry winter when he was born, telling how his life was spared. He described his teen years, his going Outside for schooling. He explained the old fears along with a detailed account of his deliverance from their harassment and bondage. He related miracles he had seen in answer to prayer. Without doubt this gentleman had the facts down pat: God cared about him, God cares about everyone. He sent Jesus to die for us. We can never be saved by our own good works, but we're saved through faith in the Lord Jesus Christ. Ours is a childlike acceptance of a gift so freely given, then turning everything over to Him and living for Him all our days. Concrete, unchangeable facts.

While listening to him speak, visitors occasionally slipped out. Motioning to fellow travelers, they urged, "Come and hear an old Eskimo who looks and talks like one of patriarchs."

A woman's voice nearly broke as she added in reverential awe, "That white-haired man has walked with God."

Walked he had, over the hills and through the valleys. And still he walked on.

While in his late seventies Patkotak again became ill. He was weary too—worn out from years of sled pulling. Despite carefully following his doctor's instructions, he simply couldn't bounce back to good health. At last he agreed to treatment at the hospital in Anchorage.

Why should he who was used to reaching out in faith for others have to take such a long trip seeking help for himself? In simple trust he chose to believe that the Lord had a reason for allowing this too. Perhaps as a bonus the Lord would also let him know why he had to go that long route. If he never knew, that was all right too.

"My radio," he smiled as he pointed to his heart, "it's tuned to Heaven all the time. When the fog settles down, I know what lies beyond the fog."

As the weeks went by he learned of patients being released and new ones being admitted. He also heard that a native woman down the hall was dying of cancer, but how does a sick man pray for somebody else? Never mind, God's Word still holds true. House-slippering down to her room, he shared his faith. Shortly afterward the cancer patient was dismissed as being in complete remission. Because of this miracle, she accepted Jesus as Lord of her life. After that Patkotak himself was able to return to his home in the north. Some time later the woman he had prayed for visited Barrow. There, before a large congregation, she told how God sent someone her way when earthly hope was

Endurance

gone. "I have no brothers or sisters from before," she concluded, "but now all who believe in Jesus are my brothers and sisters. I have a big family in the Lord."

Reflecting on the variety of spiritual adventures and valuable lessons through which his heavenly Father had proven faithful, Patkotak's furrowed face lit up. "My God is real," he reaffirmed, "and He has been so good to me."

During those, his last years, Patkotak made his home with his daughter Elizabeth. Although eventually phasing out of community functions completely, he did attend church whenever possible. If Brother Paul wasn't in his usual place, his pastor stopped by the following day to see how he was doing. Then came the sequence of Sundays when the older man no longer took his usual place at the hour of worship. He had reached the staying-home point, but the fire in his soul couldn't be put out or even reduced to embers.

"Would you like to visit Brother Paul?" a later missionary asked one of his guests. "If he knew you before, he might not recognize you now since his eyesight and memory have begun to fail. But if you would like to visit him..." his voice trailing off with that uncertain pause that lets a person know what answer he wants.

Alone in My Kayak

Once inside the house, the pastor announced in a loud voice, "Brother Paul, I'm the preacher, David Wilson. I've come to visit. I bring you company who loves Jesus too."

"Loves Jesus. Yes, yes," the old man replied unhesitatingly. "And I love Him. I sit here and I pray and remember God's Word. He has been so good to me!"

With each punctuated statement his voice took on strength. Grasping the arms of his chair, he tried to get up—all the while still talking. The younger man lent him support, but when on his feet the bent form appeared supernaturally charged as he took command of an invisible audience. His visitors? As far as Patkotak was concerned, they weren't even there.

With eyes that could barely discern objects close at hand, he looked out beyond earthly surroundings to talk about the glory of the Lord. No wonder he had to stand! Like an audience rising to its feet for the majestic strains of Handel's "Hallelujah Chorus," the veteran soldier of the Cross couldn't remain seated.

He loved to quote the psalmist David for he too never ceased being overwhelmed with the reality of his salvation, the wonder of it all. Patkotak spoke in English and in Inupiaq, reminiscing and

Endurance

rejoicing until physically exhausted. The minister, marking the old gentleman's fatigue, helped him sit down again.

A holy hush filled the room Patkotak's two friends, with heads bowed, assented inaudibly before slipping out the door. It would have been out of place to so much as whisper a good-bye, to interrupt this humble servant lost in communion with Him whom his soul loved.

"Wow!" his visitor said to herself, "he's not all here. And that's a powerful compliment!"

Patkotak's tired body begging release served him notice with increasing aches and pains. Medication intended to relieve discomfort in turn brought on undesirable side effects. His children wearied of well-meant observations: "Your father is slipping. His mind isn't clear anymore."

While accepting that such indignities can accompany failing health, they refused to accept their father's increasing memory losses as incurable. "Nothing is wrong with my dad," Simeon replied defensively. "It's the medication he's on."

He proved his point by taking his father to their summer camp where he and Susan could offer him the best of fresh fish, caribou, duck soup and whatever else he craved. Within a few days after

Alone in My Kayak

tapering off some of his prescriptions, the older Patkotak's mind cleared considerably. He regained strength enough to walk around outdoors. Sitting down to rest, he breathed deeply of fresh air, reliving highlights of the past, telling stories his grandchildren wanted to hear one more time.

Like life itself, Arctic summers are short. Shadows lengthened. Patkotak's vitality diminished accordingly, once more confining him to the house and ensuing medical attention. Elizabeth carried the added load of keeping him as comfortable as possible, preparing favorite dishes in the hopes of teasing his taste buds into action.

Finally her patient had to be flown to Anchorage again—the one place he had hoped against. After going through surgery it appeared that his sojourn on this earth was over. His mind wandered. When some of the relatives came to see him, he talked about his wife Ethel and baby Mary having been there to visit him.

"This is the end," friends thought. But not so, for to everyone's surprise Patkotak again rallied to the point of relishing the native food they brought. Best of all, he'd be released to his daughter's care after a few weeks in the convalescent center. Disappointed with the delay, he took it in stride nonetheless.

Endurance

In the rest home he appeared to be holding his own. Though his voice was weak, he could be clearly heard and understood. Perhaps there was someone else he could reach for the Lord....

When that nice nurse comes by, I'll talk to her about Jesus. I wonder if she knows Him. I must tell her how good He has been to me...tell her....

His mind was tired. Let it float away with panoramas of the past.

"Mr. Patkotak. Paul..." an attendant whispered as she touched his shoulder to arouse him. After sitting quite a while in his wheelchair, he might want something to eat, or perhaps to lie down. But he didn't respond.

Patkotak had been by himself when the summons came. No one took note of his last words. No one was there to hold his hand and to assure him that they were standing by. Family and friends would have vied for the privilege....

Was it out of keeping that this sage should die alone? Reviewing his life's story, we have to concede that he might have wanted it so, to walk those last steps by himself as he was used to doing.

Only he was too weak to walk it. He who often had quoted "underneath are the everlasting arms" leaned heavy. In this hour he would let his whole

Alone in My Kayak

weight rest on the Lord. Did it seem as if again he was placed in the snow to die and someone came along to pick him up? Someone much stronger than Grandmother, or even Aapa who had carried him over to his big sled. Picked up as if he were a little child. No fear—only peace and safety. Not really an unfamiliar experience, for he had felt that security before. He had read it in the Word too. "The beloved of the Lord shall dwell in safety by Him...between His shoulders" (Deut. 33:12).

Paul Patkotak rested. Then, lifted up from between those shoulders, his feet barely touched ground as he moved ahead with light and easy steps. Quickening his pace, he entered the North Gate shouting with vigor of eternal youth, "My God is real!"

In what other way could this man of God have gone home?

Funeral rites were held in Barrow for Paul Patkotak who left this world November 25, 1982, the day after his ninety-first birthday. Afterward adherents of both the Presbyterian and Assembly churches, along with others who never went to church at all, flew to Wainwright for a second memorial service. It had been Patkotak's wish that his body be laid to rest beside Ethel's.

They listened to an obituary, a sermon and eulogies befitting a champion of the faith. Gentle talk rustled through the neighborly crowd that assembled around a snowy grave site to pay their last respects. Like a builder who after pounding a nail securely in place gives it a final tap, first one and then another summed up Patkotak's earthly pilgrimage by a single comment: "He was right."

They understood the message that the man, through years of gentle admonition and practical application, had tried to convey.

"And now we know it," they said. "He was right."

Yes, he was right. His God is real.

Bibliography

Båtvik, Torbjørn. *Med Gud I Kajakk Og Konebåt.* Oslo, Norway: Filadelfiaforlaget a/s, 1978.

Bills, Paul. *Alaska.* Springfield, Missouri: Gospel Publishing House, 1980.

Calkins, R.H. *High Time.* Seattle, Washington: The Marine Digest Publishing Co., Inc., 1952.

Lutgen, Kurt. *Two Against the Arctic.* New York: Pantheon Books, Inc., 1957.

Rasmussen, Knud. *Across Arctic America.* New York: Greenwood Press, Publishers, 1969; orginally published in 1927 by G.P. Putnam's Sons.

Ray, Dorothy Jean. *The Eskimos of Bering Strait, 1650-1898.* Utah: University of Utah Press, 1975.

Steven, Hugh. *Good Broth to Warm Our Bones.* Westchester, Illinois: Good News Publishers, 1982.

Van Valen, William B. *Eskimoland Speaks.* Caldwell, Idaho: The Caxton Printers, Ltd., 1941.